Gaspar Pedro González

A MAYAN LIFE

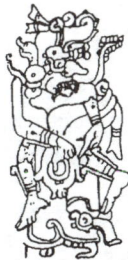

Yax Te' Foundation
1995

FIRST ENGLISH EDITION 1995
2nd Printing 1996
3rd Printing 1997
4th Printing 1999
5th Printing 2000
6th Printing 2001

Title of original: *La otra cara*

Translated by Elaine Elliott

Edited by Fernando Peñalosa and Janet Sawyer

Cover design: The day 13 Ajaw

© Gaspar Pedro González

ISBN 1-886502-01-3

YAX TE' Foundation
3520 Coolheights Drive
Rancho Palos Verdes, CA 90275-6231, U. S. A.
Tel/FAX (310) 377-8763

A Mayan Life

•

It all began when the gods inscribed their great signs on the stelae of time. It was on the day Thirteen Ajaw.

Jolomk'u, according to the stories of the grandparents, was the name of a village situated on a tall ridge among a multitude of hills and mountains. It was a colórful village, woven with the work of men and women, with their lives, illusions and failures. Cold air rode freely among the savage hills, coming face to face with the people of Jolomk'u.

In the shadow of the wings of Ajaw, the manifestation of the great God, night fell.

Soon the dark contours of the high mountains appeared like giants in the night. It was a night of a thousand centuries of history. It didn't seem to be the same wind, the same night, the same contours. It seemed that Ajaw was aging among the pines and that his hands had lost the ability to sculpt life on indecipherable stelae.

The moon, like a great eye in the night, came sailing over dark waves of sleepy clouds. It shone its great gaze at Jolomk'u. It tried to pull aside the storm clouds to cast its light on the sleeping landscape. The silhouetted mountain slopes were sprinkled with gamboling lambs. The night closed the sheepfold and then opened the door to stars flying toward the great heights like thousands of fireflies.

In the shifting lights of the evening, the men of Jolomk'u

found themselves alone. One by one they lit pitch pine slivers in the huts, until the village was full of the spattering of smoking firebrands that made the crickets cry. A chorus of dogs barked, intoning their protests against the unannounced strange rustling noises of the *nawales*, the local evil spirits, terrifying the living, coming out to prowl over their realm.

Along the roads some girls out late with their clay water pots ran furtively toward the spring for a fleeting encounter with their boyfriends hiding in the thickets.

A brook ran down quietly through the village, spraying watercress, nightshade and water, mint and water into the open mouths of the amorous girls' water pots. There, right by the bend of the brook, before it hastened over the precipice and ran through a small plain on the highest part of Jolomk'u, Mekel had built his little wattle-and-daub house with a straw roof and oak posts, from which hung armadillo shells.

In the stillness of that night, Mekel's wife, Lotaxh, struggled with birth pangs. She was alone in the house, in a cold sweat, the drops of pain like an approaching rainstorm.

When Mekel arrived and put down his load of firewood, he found his wife gripping one of the posts. He didn't know if he felt happiness, pity or sorrow coursing through his veins. What he was sure of was that his son would arrive this night, clinging to the fingers of Ajaw.

"Go call Ewul. It's time," said Lotaxh. Mekel put on his light sandals with their soles made of tire treads, took his machete and set off with his *capixay* jacket on his shoulder toward the nearby village where Ewul lived. He ran like a deer, jumping over the underbrush, taking shortcuts, racing over the paths, climbing the slopes until he arrived at the waterfall, beyond the great rocks, almost to the edge of the pine groves where the virgin forest began.

"Hello there," cried out Mekel in front of the little straw-covered house. A dog barked lazily, accustomed to the midwife's numerous daily visitors.

"Yes" answered a woman's voice from inside the hut.

"It's me, doña Ewul. I came to get you because my wife's labor pains started around midday," he said.

"All right, just a moment. You should have told me sooner. Malku," called the woman, "Get me artemisia and *pericón* herbs, chicken fat and the bottle of liquor. Hurry, because we may get there too late."

Mekel wiped his sweaty forehead and neck with the sleeve of his *capixay*.

Meanwhile in Jolomk'u, Lotaxh, a young woman accustomed to pain and work, with strong arms like a grinding stone, grasped one of the pine stakes attached to one corner of the pole bed. Her survival instincts had led her to prepare an adequate place for her child to be born in case she did not have the midwife's help. She had stretched a straw mat over the earth and some old clothes on the mat, forming a nest. On one side the fire was like an eye slowly shutting an ashen lid. Some chickens complained under the pole bed because Lotaxh's moans kept them awake. In the lulls between waves of pain, she pondered, "My God, I hope that the fox's howl I heard this morning isn't a bad omen." Unraveling like a skein of thread in her mind were the advice and instructions of the women she had spoken with regarding childbirth.

Outside the hut the cold was intense, but Lotaxh was still sweating, sinking her fingernails into the trunk and tearing off the bark. Three hours had passed and the laboring woman's strength was waning, just like the dying flames.

A candle hanging from the sooty walls flickered, begging for more fuel, before it was swallowed up by the invading darkness.

It seemed that everything was coming to an end. Her pale face was like a tender avocado leaf, her breath sometimes quickening and sometimes imperceptible. Her eyes saw everything spinning around: the candle dying, the hearth spinning, the barks always more distant. She was about to lose consciousness, curled up on her straw mat on the hard soil of black clay, when Mekel came in all out of breath and sweaty. The steam rose from his body through the holes in his shirt like the vapors of the sweat bath.

A little while later, Ewul arrived accompanied by a boy about ten years old, her helper in the preparation of medicines and incense.

"Leave me alone with her," she said to Mekel.

The boy began to make a fire in a smaller hut outside. He made some beverages from the herbs that he carried in his bag, first using the chicken fat along with the bottle of liquor.

Mekel put on his *capixay* to calm his nerves, which he found difficult to control. He blew on the fire with all his might to get some light. He didn't want to think in the dark, because specters with unpleasant faces appeared out of the darkness. He spoke to the boy in order to feel less alone, but he did not answer. He hunkered down to listen to the night tiptoeing like the brook that ran beside his house.

A long time went by. The moon had changed position. The morning frost had fallen. A cry shattered the great silence, crashing against Mekel's pricked-up ears. It shattered the chicken's sleep under the pole beds, reverberated in the alert ears of the nodding dogs, shook the thousand-year-old mountains, and ran through the nerve centers of all of Jolomk'u.

A boy had been born.

Ewul was a woman about fifty years old, hair still black, few signs of the passage of time on her face, large flat feet with calluses caused by so much squatting on the straw mats, firm hands used to holding the naked first-fruit of the women of that region. She took the infant in her hands, cut the umbilical cord, cleaned it as a matter of professional routine and wrapped the child in diapers made of Mekel's old pants and Lotaxh's *güipiles*. Then she wrapped the child in an old wool *capixay* whose stiff hairs made the child cry when he felt them against his delicate skin. He was a Maya, so he needed to become accustomed to discomfort right from the start. The midwife continued her work. She formed the head, giving it a round shape like a lump of clay. She went over the curve of the nose, the fingers, the arms, the legs and the placement of the fontanel. Then she put a round red cap on him and drawing him close to her, she blew mouth to mouth, three breaths that came from the roots of Ewul's lungs, of all of the Mayas of all ages, drawn from the root of time like a symbol of the life and the inheritance of the ancestors.

The child cried apprehensively, his body shaking in the cold-filled night. The cry reverberated across the valleys, and through the canyon gorges. It went snaking among the huts, and withdrew into distant time, searching out its origins in his first ancestor's initial cry of pain.

Ewul went out to spread the word that everything had gone well. She asked for censing: coals and incense to send smoke throughout the house. She smoked a corn-husk cigarette to soothe her throat after work well done. She spoke hardly at all.

That same night on the headboard of the mother and her son were hung the tools appropriate for a successful adult life: machete, ax, hoe, carrying strap, rope. Everything that a man needed in Jolomk'u.

Lotaxh fell into a deep sleep. It was dawn and the others had settled down to sleep where they could, warming the stretch of cold earth under their ribs with the weight of their tiredness, like a daily rehearsal for death and intimate union with the earth. The bubbling of a clay pot on the hearthstones was the only thing that could be heard when dawn came to the house. Almost everyone slept. Mekel was the only one still working. The gnarled feet of a dark-fleshed rooster poked out of the pot, which kept boiling on the hearthstones.

Next to the fire he warmed his thoughts like swaddling clothes to wrap his firstborn.

With the first rays of dawn some women arrived with small gifts of food. Those that came empty-handed, because they found nothing to bring from their empty bowls, washed clothes, went to the spring for water, swept the house, washed dishes, cooked food. The men brought firewood. Some brought a few pounds of corn or beans as a gesture of support.

A large firecracker had announced the birth, spread by word of mouth way beyond the edges of the village. Family members and neighbors arrived in haste, shaking the sleep off their feet. The grandfathers, grandmothers, aunts and uncles, godparents and friends all arrived. There was a party at Mekel's.

As the symbolic source of life and breath of many children of that region, the midwife drew on her authority to announce in official tones before all those present the news that hung like a question mark over the people.

"We give thanks to God Our Father because he has blessed this family with the birth of a male son without complications," she said.

Smiles blossomed on those faces, teeth showing like white corn, breaking out in the laughter of the collective joy.

The eldest man of the family, relieved of the numbness of the cramps in his joints, wearing a red kerchief on his head, and holding a cane made from a twisted root, got up to approach the hearth. He dug a hole under the ashes and without saying a word, wrapped up something in *kanac* leaves, tied it up with a bit of corn husk and then covered it by tossing the ashes over it. It was the newborn's umbilical cord.

Thirteen Ajaw had left his realm. Now it was One Imox, the sacred day for improving family life, neighborly relations and work. It is also a good day to pray to God for health, life and work. That day there was a family council to plan the celebration of the first festival in honor of the newborn: *ox q'in*, which should take place the third day after birth. It involved the selection of the child's godparents and the selection of the logically predetermined name, that of the paternal grandfather, as the parents well knew. Another matter that would have to be taken care of was registering the birth at the town hall.

The scribe, or *ajtz'ib'*, was the most trusted person in the community, not only because of his ability to read and write but also because of his friendships with Ladinos. For these reasons, Mekel asked him to go to town with him to obtain a birth certificate for the child.

They left Jolomk'u long before the sun showed its face at the gateway to the horizon. Before the offices opened they were waiting their turn in the hallway. The morning air combed the tops of the bushes that grew in the town square. Every once in a while a man entrusted with telling time would strike a bell hanging in front of the town hall eight times.

"The offices are about to open," commented the scribe, talking to himself.

Forty-five more minutes went by and people began arriving at the town hall for various reasons: disputes, land division, domestic quarrels, permits for cutting trees, or complaints of Ladino cheating. Then the town secretary was seen coming down one of the cobblestone streets, a mournful figure in black *capixay* and pants, his tight belt making him look like a gourd divided in two and tied in the middle with a cord. He was a man getting moldy among the books of that old town hall. He had been the secretary since time immemorial and knew his way through all the maze of those books and of his calling, especially the daily chores.

"Good morning, Mr. Secretary," greeted Mekel, hat in hand.

The man went into his office without acknowledging Mekel, leaving behind him the stench of tobacco, although he did not carry any lighted cigarette at that moment. It was like the odor of those shelves of old books.

Mekel wanted to go in, but a confrontational policeman with a scar on his face from a machete wound, stopped him by pushing him out.

"Come back another day. Today the secretary isn't going to see anybody," he said. "Didn't you know that today is Columbus Day? It's a holiday," he concluded.

"But, it's that ..." began the scribe.

"You stupid Indian, didn't I tell you today is a holiday?"

Actually, that day was just one among many that the local authorities had declared to be a holiday.

Returning to their village, the scribe and Mekel were commenting that they would undoubtedly be fined for not having applied for the birth certificate within the stipulated time. Mekel, who was not well informed about such matters, asked his companion:

"What holiday is this Columbus Day, sir?"

"Friend Mekel, to us Mayas many things have not been revealed. Our world is not the world of the Ladinos; our holidays are not their holidays; our lives develop along different lines. We don't have the same vision of life: theirs is one way and ours another. Race, nationality or so-called national identity, means belonging to something or to a group, to be part of it, do you understand?"

"Yes, I understand."

After a holiday it was customary for the town officials to replace their lost energy and cure their headaches with another day off.

Days later, they went to the mayor's office to try again. They weren't allowed to go into the town secretary's smoky office until after midday, when the sun had changed its angle and the roosters announced the time with a song to the wind. There were a lot of people in the corridors waiting their turn, swallowing their boredom with yawns. Mekel, hat in hand, nervously approached the secretary.

"Good afternoon," he said. At his side stood the scribe.

"What do you want?" asked the secretary churlishly.

"Sir," said the scribe, "A few days ago this man's wife gave birth to a son. Exactly five days ago," he said.

"And why did you wait until now to register the birth?"

"Sir, you yourself told us it was a holiday," said Mekel.

"That's not my fault. To get the kid's birth certificate you have to bring three sheets of legal paper, the midwife's identity card; the father's identity card and his signature or two witnesses, if he's unable to sign his name. Oh yes! I forgot to tell you that since more than three days have elapsed, there'll be a charge of five quetzales per day, you know."

"But sir, we're very poor," Mekel began.

"That's your problem, the law is the law."

The *ajtz'ib'* intervened, saying that they had run out of legal paper in town, but that they were willing to pay the value of the paper and as far as the identity card of the midwife was concerned, she was a Mayan woman, and so she didn't have such a document.

"Why didn't you look for someone in town, like from the health center?" asked the secretary.

"Sir, our long-standing custom is that it should be someone from our own people, because we have certain ceremonies that others don't know how to perform. Our women don't trust outsiders. Everyone is born like this."

The secretary used his imagination astutely in order to think up a pretext to inflate the final bill. Pretending to be benevolent with the worried villagers, he pulled out an old book, opened it like the leaves of old squeaky doors and began to thumb through it. He pretended to study the legal possibilities of that complicated case like a serious legal eagle.

"You're the father of the boy?" he asked Mekel.

"Yes, sir," he answered hastily.

"What name are you going to give him?" he asked.

"Well, we want to give him my dad's name, according to our customs. What do you think?"

"Oh no! Forget that foolishness. That's why we have an almanac." Having said that, he went up to a calendar hanging on the wall, dirty from being touched so much, and looked for the date of birth and then said: "It was the day of St. Serapius. But if you insist on giving him your father's name, then we'll have to make certain legal arrangements," he said.

"Please, Mr. secretary, we want to name him Lwin and his father is named Mekel, so that his name would be Pedro Miguel," interposed the scribe.

"Well, I'll do everything I can for you, but it's just one more thing, and you know that it's not easy to change the law. Wait outside."

After a boring hour Mekel and his companion were called in. The secretary read in a Spanish that limped into Mekel's ears, the paper with the name of Lwin Mekel, changed to Pedro Miguel for the Ladinos, planted like his umbilical cord. It was one more link in the line of Lwins and Mekels from Jolomk'u. The secretary finished reading and brought Mekel a stamp pad, took his stiffened right thumb, lifted it, and led it like a blind man to stamp his thumb print on the paper that he had just read.

"Well, son," he said in an affable tone, "It's all set."

"Thank you, Mr. secretary. Excuse me, how much is it?" asked Mekel.

"Well, for you, and considering that the elections are coming up, I'll ask for a little help. Let me have twenty-five bucks."

Mekel, putting his hat on the floor, looked down into his string shoulder bag, pulled out a knotted handkerchief and took out a few bills. Before counting them one by one, he spit on his fingers so that not a single one would escape his count. He managed to scrape together the twenty-five with the change that lay piled on top of the bills.

"Next!" said the secretary.

The second day after Lwin's birth, Two Iq', had been the day to look for godparents for the child. Mekel, the father, along with the paternal grandparents made a journey that evening to the village where lived Maltin Nolaxh and his wife Lolen Tumaxh, who had been selected as the godparents.

The sun was falling like a great comet over the crests of the mountains that surrounded Jolomk'u, when the small retinue set out, carrying small bundles of pitch pine to light their return, and each carrying a machete like an extra limb. Over the narrow road, actually nothing more than a path, they went one after another, one woman stumbling barefoot behind the men. They had to hurry, because the night was quickly swallowing up the day. They took shortcuts to reach the mountain and arrive quickly at their destination. There they found some workers returning to their huts for the night, who greeted them as they passed by. On their backs they were carrying firewood with their tools on top, all supported by carrying straps across their foreheads. Nearby, a lover whistled a melancholy tune like an evening serenade for some girl from the neighborhood, putting all his emotion into the sad whistle. The group devoured the paths with their callused feet, accustomed to conquering long distances. They passed groups of adobe houses that kept them company along the way. Some dogs came out to bark at them there, jealously guarding their territory, the owners quieting them by throwing at them whatever was within reach. After responding to the travelers' greetings, the people returned hurriedly to the hearth that gave them warmth and smoke under the straw roofs. Their comfort was to sit on hard three-legged benches, stir up the fire, clean the chiles in the depths of a clay bowl and smear them on hot tortillas to make them tasty. Their eyes watered on account of the chile, which stimulated their hunger and made them devour the corn tortillas. But above all their tears were over the lack of opportunity to change the disagreeable situation in which they spent their lives.

Inside the hut, the travellers heard the slap, slap of women's hands making tortillas to fill the stomachs of their crying children, struggling to keep their eyes open in the smoke.

The grandmother lagged behind the group, as her feet were losing the habit and the ability to conquer the road. The years weighed on her steps. They sat down to wait for her on the edge of the road, which was now only dimly seen in the night. It was the highest part of the mountain and they pulled out their cigarettes of corn husks to fill their dry mouths with smoke and saliva, and allow the grandmother time to get back her strength. They sat on some rocks like fireflies as they lit and then snuffed out their cigarettes. At their feet the village appeared like stars fallen from the sky. Each little hut was a light that came on, each home smoky with crying children.

"Let's go on," said the grandmother.

"Shall I light the pitch pine?" asked Mekel.

"No, not for me," she said. "This old lady sees better at night than in the day," she said.

Upon entering the hamlet, they were welcomed by dogs that came out to bark, setting off all the dogs of the neighborhood.

Mekel banged his machete against a stick or a rock to scare away the animals that would not leave the strangers alone. Arriving at their destination they called:

"Hello there."

"Who is it?"

"Good evening, it's us."

A maimed dog, which had its tail and ears mutilated so that it wouldn't get rabies, threatened them so loudly that it was impossible to hear. He rushed forth impetuously until the owner threw a rock to drive him off amidst growling and barking.

"Come on in. We're sorry the animals have bothered you and almost bitten you. We've been giving chile to that poor dog and that's why he's gotten so mean."

After greeting the people in the house, they sat down on the little wooden benches offered them, taking places around the hearth, which projected light and heat. They invited the grandmother to take her place next to the women near the grinding stone, facing the men. She sat on a mat next to the women. There was a woman attached to the grinding stone as though it were all of one piece with her, moving rhythmically, using the stone to crush the grains, which became a soft dough, which able hands then made into round lumps. These would end up on a griddle which cast an eclipse from the fire over the people. The griddle, a real bright red, cooked the round bubbly tortillas like craters on a big full moon. Cigarette smoke was flying, and the conversation was animated, touching on the work, scarcity and poverty which filled their lives. During pauses in the conversation, one could hear the crunch, crunch of the grinding stone .

Maltin Nolaxh stirred the fire, pushing pieces of burning, smoking wood under the clay griddle, which was supported by the hearth stones. Between the hearthstones were the simmering pots of black bean soup and thick corn gruel. Corn, beans and chile—linked through time in long chains of generations eating only corn, beans and chile. From time to time, they varied the routine with wild vegetables: *colinabos*, nightshade, amaranth and watercress.

The basket was filled with tortillas, hot off the griddle. The woman brought a clay pot with warm water for people to wash their hands. The host invited the visitors to make use of the water, which went from hand to hand, followed by a little bit of water to rinse out their mouths, which they spat into the corners of the house. They dried their hands on their coat sleeves or on their mended pants, which had patches over the patches. They held the clay pots with beans at the bottom with one hand and with the other they emptied the basket of hot tortillas, which increased the heat of the chile in their mouths.

"Eat, take some of our Mother Corn, please," said the host from time to time. They blew on their hands as though they were gaining strength each time they took the tortillas, as a sign of respect to Mother Corn.

"Thank you," they answered, "here we are eating our sacred corn, thank you very much," they repeated.

A child who had been nodding as he slept over in a corner awoke. Crying, he timidly went to lie down on his mat, which was stretched out in the corner. Tattered blankets with holes in them were stretched over the slumbering child, blankets where the cold of the night went in and out. That child was not the exception, but rather was representative of the life of Jolomk'u and all the Mayan villages of the region.

Upon finishing supper they gave thanks to one another with their hands together, emphasizing with burps how satisfied and full they were and how appreciative of the family's services.

"Thank you," they said. "May God bless you."

"I hope you've eaten well, that you're not still hungry. It's your own fault if you didn't eat enough," insisted the hosts.

"We've eaten. Our Mother Corn knows that we don't disdain her. You are very kind."

Once more they passed around the little bowl of lukewarm water to rinse out their mouths. Again they touched the firebrands to the ends of their corn husk cigarettes, and men and women let out smoke through their mouths and noses. Then the visitors began explaining the purpose of their late night visit. The grandfather of the newborn, a man with a face lined by the years, with two scanty wisps of whiskers that came down like moss over his trembling lips, was the one who passed out the cigarettes. He passed the smoking brand to each one and waited for each one to light his cigarette. Waiting for the appropriate moment, he spit vigorously, making an arc in the air and then spoke:

"The great God that holds up the four corners of the world, like pillars of the universe, who is with us in nature and gives life by the air we breathe, light by Father Sun, life by Mother Earth and water, has permitted a male child be born to my son and his wife, under the protection of our father Thirteen Ajaw. Considering our poverty and humble condition, we have decided to ask you to have pity on us and accept the responsibility of being godparents to our little grandson, because of your exemplary life and your friendship with our family," said the old man.

"Don Maltin, doña Lolen," interrupted the grandmother, "forgive us if on some occasion we haven't shown you all the respect you deserve. Perhaps our children have not greeted you on the road or have not doffed their hat to you, or our animals have trespassed onto your cornfield or your land. These are situations beyond our control. Forgive us. We've chosen you because you are ordinary folks like us, and your example will serve as a guide to our grandchild."

"We're really happy that the child was born without any problems and that the mother has recovered satisfactorily," said Maltin Nolaxh. "Really, there's no dearth of problems and complications, especially in such cases. Above all, if it is the first child, the mother has to be very careful not to go uncovered, nor to touch cold water until she has bathed in the sweat bath. As far as being godparents to the child, we appreciate your choosing us very much. Our merits are very limited, but we can't refuse the honor you do us, for our elders' tradition tells us that it's our duty to accept with pleasure. My wife and I thank you."

"In view of the fact that you have done us the great favor of agreeing to be the child's godparents, a thousand thanks from us," said Mekel, "and according to our customs, we'll expect you tomorrow in our home to celebrate the child's *ox q'in* in a simple way."

The night was gnawing away at time like rats gnawing on ears of corn stored in an attic. They spoke of the care of the child and of the mother: eye diseases, avoiding hot-blooded people, who should not see the baby, what herbs to prepare for the sweat bath, the incense in the corners to scare away the *nawales* so they couldn't take over the child's soul, the clothing that shouldn't be left out in the night air to avoid frightening the newborn, the warming of the head, the tying of the feet and hands of the little one so he would be a calm man in the future, avoiding, if possible, getting near pregnant women, drunks, or overheated people. At night they should leave crosses made of pitch pine behind the doors, tie a bag of seven herbs wrapped in red cloth around the neck of the child, and tie the navel so that it won't pop out when he cries, and thus in his adult life he will be able to carry heavy loads in his daily work. They should give the mother enough artemisia, *alucema*, *pericón*, and chicken soup with lots of mint. Furthermore, she shouldn't lack chile at each meal for warmth and cups of boiled yellow corn meal, so that she would have plenty of milk for the child day and night, until he reached the age of two. To keep the little one from vomiting, it was recommended that the mother should drink a cup of liquor from time to time, which would also avoid indigestion.

Before going to bed they lit pitch pine torches dripping with turpentine. Then they said good-bye and opened a path through the dense night. The dogs that were beginning to fall asleep, coiled up on their flanks, suddenly stretched out, and started to bark in a contagious chorus of protest.

There were three celebrations in honor of each person in

Jolomk'u. *Ox q'in* was the first, and it was held the third day
after birth to give thanks for life to the great God.

Relatives, neighbors, and friends began to get together at
Mekel's house. Happiness shone across their faces, a respite
from the daily work and pain. They momentarily left their
sorrow, their struggle, and their exhaustion hanging in their
houses. The men brought firewood, corn and beans. The
women offered their empty hands to do housework. They
slaughtered chickens, washed the new mother's clothes, blew
like bellows on the sleepy fires under the griddles, ground
corn on the stone, or made tortillas near the fire like a
perpetually applauding audience.

All wore tattered but clean clothes instead of the tattered
work clothes left on their beds. They welcomed each man as
he noisily dropped off his load of firewood in the patio and
wiped off his sweat, and gave him a small cup of coffee made
of toasted corn with brown sugar. Real coffee was drunk only
when one went to work at the fincas. On one side were the
men, on the other the women. Conversations developed
regarding their daily work, sick relatives, the harvest, and
trucks full of people falling into ravines.

The women blew like bellows on the fire. The children
cried endlessly, fussy from so much smoke. The older ones
ran around happily outdoors, knowing that they would eat
well that day. Finally, after so long there would be meat,
something whose taste they had forgotten. They ran from one
side to the other, their hunger awakened by the smell of the
boiling pots. They entered to look furtively at the pots on the
hearthstones, went running out again, dreaming of chewing
on a bone or eating a bowl of soup.

Inside the house they set up rustic planks to serve as seats
for the guests. People kept arriving and those that didn't fit
inside stayed outside. In one corner, the mother, with her head
tied in a white kerchief, was lying down with the child. She
had changed her clothes too. She had put on the white *güipil*

that she used on Sundays to go to town, along with her marbled wraparound skirt, and a checkered cloth as protection against the cold. For the first time, her son was wearing diapers, made from Mekel's old pants. His colorful hand-woven cap with a design dominated by red, and so good for protecting newborns from the evil eye, was closed at the crown like the peaks of the straw roofs.

Ox q'in was the public presentation of the newborn. No one else had met him yet except his mother and the midwife.

At the crossroads near the entrance to the house they had built an arch with *pacaya* leaves and green pine boughs adorned with wild flowers hung according to Mayan aesthetics. The children were delighted with their job as watchmen, playing around as they waited under the large arch full of *patas de gallo* and other flowers. One of the children ran to announce the news: "The godparents are here." Actually, the couple was just then coming down the path that went across the river.

"Tie up the dogs," someone suggested. The dogs had actually been tied up since dawn.

Mekel went out to receive the godparents under the arch, without letting go of his machete. The women milled around doing housework, the children ran from one side to another, the grandparents raised themselves lazily on their arthritic legs, relying on the strength of their canes. After the exchange of greetings between the godparents and the family, they came into the house. On a rustic table were some candles with restless flames in front of wooden crosses. There was a pot without ears stuffed with flowers of all colors.

The new arrivals went discretely to the crosses, which had a picture of the Sacred Heart on one side and a Virgin with Child on the other side. The images could barely be made out under the layer of smoke and time. They kneeled down and, after kissing the earth, brought two large candles out of a bag, passed them in front of the crosses and the saints, muttering prayers through their teeth. After a short while they got up and went to the corner where the mother and child were, surrounded by the torn blankets that warmed their cold nights. They greeted Lotaxh and exchanged a few routine remarks and then went to their place on the planks that served as chairs. The *ajtz' ib'*, the midwife, the diviner, and the paternal and maternal grandparents were seated there along with some neighbors and friends. It was a good opportunity to demonstrate the esteem and unity of the community. While they waited for the food, they passed the time discussing events of interest to the group. The diviner commented that this year there wouldn't be enough rain and that the cornfields wouldn't produce the needed harvests, and consequently, the price of a measure of corn would probably double.

The midwife found it alarming that the nurses of the public health centers were requiring pregnant women to attend classes on birth control. In order to get rations of corn, oil, milk, as well as medical attention for their children, they had to participate in these programs and use various methods contrary to their usual customs. And they suspected that the products they were given contained something to sterilize them so they would have no more children.

"They are always inventing new techniques for doing away with us," said the *ajtz' ib'*. "Over time, and one way or another they try to negate our existence, either physically or culturally. If you consider all the health, education, agriculture, and "development" programs, they are nothing more than instruments of alienation and a pretext for getting big loans from other countries. A friend who knows a lot about this told me not long ago that our great-great-grandchildren will already be in debt before they are born. They never take into account what we really need, nor do they ask us what we want and how we want them to do things."

No one else felt like expressing an opinion after hearing the *ajtz' ib'*, and, to change the subject, the paternal grandfather stood up with his hands clasped together and said:

"We thank God, who is the sole owner of our lives, who has kept us alive this morning and I'd like to thank you who are with us. Please have a tortilla."

"Thank you," everyone said.

"Have some food, Lotaxh," said the godmother. "Put lots of chile on your food so your milk won't get cold."

The adults ate inside the house, the children on the porch, climbing up on the stacks of firewood or on the ground, whatever way they could get comfortable enough to enjoy that chicken soup with its wings or necks that they sucked clean. One woman began to serve seconds on soup. Most bowls were filled and there was a pile of tortillas for each group of people. The mothers masticated for the smallest ones, who opened their mouths like baby birds getting their lumps of food.

It was a motley group of people dispelling their hunger. The women who hadn't found straw mats sat on their feet talking to one another.

"Please eat," the hosts repeated again and again.

The people held their clay dishes on their knees with both hands, raising them to their mouths. The hot chile made their tongues curl.

"How did you get the chickens for this party?" the midwife asked the group of women eating in a corner. "Where we live, nobody has even one chicken."

"You poor things," said another woman. "That's because of the disease that came through here about two years ago, and if it starts up again, it's almost sure to wipe out our animals one more time."

"Well, if it's a disease, one can accept it," said the godmother.

"So it wasn't coyotes or foxes?" asked the others with interest.

"No, it wasn't sickness or animals, it was people."

"But a thief couldn't steal the chickens of a whole village," they said.

"It wasn't a thief. It was one of those men that work for some institution, supposedly to improve the production and quality of our animals and harvests. One day they arrived and assembled the whole community, and we even fed them for two days, and as you know they don't just eat vegetables. We had to make donations for meat, coffee and bread. They said they had come to vaccinate our animals to avoid this disease you're talking about. We gladly took our chickens, ducks, and turkeys the day of the vaccination to the front of the town hall annex. You should have heard the animals cry, it was just like a market day. To begin with, the expert arrived around eleven in the morning. Someone had brought him on a horse, since he wouldn't dream of walking. First they vaccinated the cattle, then the dogs and pigs and finally the poultry. They put some drops in each eye of the birds and after lunch we all went home happily with our animals. What a shock the next day when we saw our birds walking around blind, running into things. They lurched from side to side as if they had been hit on the head. What had happened was that they had gone blind from the drops they put in their eyes. We didn't know whether to kill them or wait for the medicine to wear off. We were all crying at seeing our animals unable to eat. Some hand fed them and made them drink medicine, but the animals stayed blind. We went to talk to the development man of our village who understands our language, but he said the men had already gone back to the city and that they were a group of students that were studying I don't know what. The development man said they probably gave the wrong medicine or gave too much.

The women paused quietly, their thoughts traveling the stretch between heart and mind, between feelings and ideas in those simple people.

After a long while someone spoke: "At home we've talked

about this" he said. "Probably the things that are done to us are intentionally planned, or else nobody cares whether we get ahead, since the meaningless little things they come to give us just don't measure up to our needs. Or it could be that they send for things from other countries for us, and since we're so far away from any urban center, they send us people without knowledge and experience to come and do their internships or in some cases they send them as punishment to these places. The truth is that in general, whatever experts come here have come without much of a desire to work. For example: The interns come to do experiments here, and then they go to the cities to exploit people."

"Don't you think that after so many years of the same old thing, with the same promises, that the money spent to support the institutions, well used, would have made our communities grow?" suggested another. "For example, our traditional methods give better corn harvests than the famous 'demonstration plots' of the experts who say they have studied for I don't know how many years."

"My son, who understands a little Spanish," said another woman, "heard on the radio about millions in aid and loans that good people from other countries send. But from this, all we get around here is the news ."

General laughter from the men brought them back to reality, and they realized that everyone had finished eating. The hostess told her helpers to wrap up the meat left over on each plate in *kanac* leaves and to give them to the guests so they could take them home. The godparents' plates were taken to the kitchen, because for them there would be special food. The godparents stood up in their respective places and spoke to all those present: "We would like to thank you, all the good friends, the diviner, the scribe, the midwife, all of you. Thank you for the food. May God bless you."

Meanwhile the grandmother hurriedly helped Lotaxh prepare the child to be presented to everyone, since until now no one had seen him, with the exception of his mother and the midwife.

The first thing hung around his neck was the red bag containing seven herbs against the evil eye. On the wrist of his right hand they placed a coral bracelet, then the grandmother made a cross of saliva on his forehead. Without taking off the homemade cap with the red fringe, she wrapped him in a checkered cloth. Lotaxh stood up, and taking the child in her arms, went to show him to the godparents.

The godmother took him in her arms. The firecracker that went off at that moment shook the nerves of the newborn, who trembled in the godmother's arms, turning purple from crying, and looking as if his breath were gone.

The people who were outside came to see the ceremony and meet the child. Momentarily there was a crowd of people inside the house. The godparents came near the place sacred to the hybrid faith of the men of Jolomk'u, where candles were burning and the cross had arms outstretched between saints with foreign faces, to the place where the men of Jolomk'u practiced *costumbre*. The godmother cradled the child in her arms while the godfather held the incense burner in his hands, swinging the smoke that enveloped the child.

The child was presented to the crosses, to the saints, to the fire, to the beams, to the roof and to each and every part of the house. There was a murmur among the people watching the ceremony. The smell of incense was everywhere in the smoke. The godfather lifted the child to show him to the crowd. He made the sign of the cross in the air, made another sign of the cross over Mother Earth, from west to east and from north the south.

The child's crying brought them back to the reality of the here and now:

"I've seen that your little head has two whorls," continued the godfather. "The strength of Mother Nature and of the ancestors is with you. You are predestined for service," he concluded.

The godmother picked him up and took out some new clothing from the bag she carried: a red colored cap, a kerchief, a little shirt. She put them on her godchild.

Two porters accompanied the godparents after they said good-bye that afternoon. One of the boys carried a heavy basket containing bread, party tamales, meat and brown sugar. The other carried a pot full of soup and more meat. Their lithe bodies moved along the trail without raising dust, and their minds were agile, thanks to the *chicha*.

After the godparents left, the women prepared the sweat bath, that began to emit smoke through its little opening, waiting for the new mother to be purified.

No Mayan home, no matter how small, failed to have a sweat bath, attached like a callus to feet, a mound with a little door for people to enter on their knees.

It was the place were men, women, and children bathed themselves in heat. Beneath the center of the sweat bath's low vault there was a pile of a certain kind of stones which would not burst with the heat, or turn to lime in the high temperatures to which they were subjected. At first, clouds of smoke came out of the opening of the bath, but when all the wood was burned up, only the red-hot stones remained with pots of boiling water. Various wild herbs were used in the steam.

Four men carried Lotaxh on a blanket to the door of the sweat bath. She was received by two women who were already inside getting it ready. The heat was unbearable, the stones red-hot, the coals like brilliant sunsets shining in that oven. The men closed the door with a board to prevent the heat from escaping.

"Well *kumare*," said one of the women. "Put water on the rocks and I'll fan it with the leaf." Right away the rocks were sprinkled, turning the water to hot steam, filling the small enclosure with a burning mist. The three women sweated until their body juices broke out all over from their pores.

The other woman slapped her back, stroked her stomach, and massaged Lotaxh's hips with the medicinal herbs. The third time they put the water on the still red-hot stones, they burst like erupting volcanoes. Then with warm water and lard soap they bathed Lotaxh between the two of them.

"All right, boys," instructed one of the women. Without looking inside, the men quickly handed her a sheet with which to wrap Lotaxh.

"Lower her carefully," ordered the midwife.

Lotaxh was almost unconscious. The four men put her down on the blanket again, covered her over and carried her to a corner inside the house. Then they gave her a little water with anise, and she slept on her straw mat the rest of the afternoon.

●●●

One morning Mekel came down from the attic, after having figured out how much corn there was lying there on the rafters like skeletal ribs, and stood pensive and worried at the threshold of the house.

"Something is bothering you, Mekel," said his wife, who was holding Lwin in her arms. "I've noticed for several days now; it's as if your mind and body are disconnected. What's the matter?"

"If you looked in the attic and saw how little corn we have left and went out on the patio and heard the cries of the pigs, chickens, and dogs, you'd understand why I am so worried," he answered. "We're barely entering the time of scarcity, and it's going to last around five months."

The animals outside were noisily begging for food. A cat wove in and out of Lotaxh's footsteps, never leaving her alone; the pigs squealed loudly in their pens; the pesky chickens were everywhere; the dogs never stopped barking.

What worried Mekel the most was the mortgage on his land. Every day more interest accumulated. He spent his nights thinking about that, and when the roosters crowed, he was already awake turning his problems around and around in his head.

One afternoon as he was shelling corn in the patio, surrounded by his hungry animals, he suggested a plan to his wife, as she nursed the child with a cloth tied on his head.

"I should go earn some money at the fincas like the others do, so we can solve our financial problems," he began. "I'll have to talk to the labor contractor to see if they'll take me to harvest coffee or cotton in some finca. You can stay at my parent's house to take care of the child and the animals, as well as our field work until the corn harvest."

"Before deciding anything," she advised, "we should consult the diviner, so he can counsel us as to what would be best. You know, a lot of people travel to those places, and many of them don't come back. And if they come back, it's only to bury their loved ones or spend time in bed waiting to die. This worries me." said Lotaxh. "As for me, if you go I won't be idle. I've been working since I was four years old; all of my life I've worked hard. I'll take charge of the planting, care for the cornfield and the animals and especially take care of our child. I don't want to be a burden on your parents. I'll stay here and take care of the house and continue with the daily routine. I'll persuade my parents to let my little ten-year-old sister come and stay with me."

The next day Mekel's wife prepared a few tortillas and some refried beans and wrapped them up in a napkin to take to the old diviner.

They walked along mountain ridges and dusty roads, forging ahead despite their weariness. On reaching the crest of a hill, they saw the diviner's house in the distance, smoking below the horizon.

"It's about two leagues more," figured Mekel, without knowing for certain what a league was. It was a way of saying, "Let's go on, it's not much farther."

This house, like all the others, had a dog baring his fangs at the visitors. Behind the smoky door appeared a woman with tangled hair, bearing on her body strips of rags like a tree hung with moss. The woman mechanically shooed away the dog with the mistrustful gaze, which settled on its side in the thicket, spitting out insults at random.

She pointed to some logs, as though inviting them to wait their turn. She didn't give them time to explain or ask for the old man. It was presumed that they had come to consult him regarding some problem. The woman turned around and was swallowed up again by the smoky mouth of the house. From inside the smoke came the voice of a woman tearfully asking what to do about her husband, who had been drinking for three weeks.

Following the woman on her way out, the diviner walked with limbs swollen from sitting so long. Bent over his cane, he stopped to urinate behind a pumpkin vine, which looked like a tangle of green threads on a loom.

Bent over under the weight of his ninety years, the marks of time were etched on his face. The tufts of his yellowish mustache hung like a goat's beard over the edges of his mouth. Under his bristling eyebrows two small penetrating eyes shone out from the wrinkles on his face. He had tied a red kerchief around his grubby head. As he returned, he signaled to the couple to follow him inside. The ragged woman kneeled among the ashes, trying to revive the fire to erase the smoke. At a signal from the old man, she filled a small bowl with tobacco mixed with lime. He grabbed a handful and raised it to his mouth and kept chewing, which produced a great deal of saliva. His spit had marked two meters of ground all around him.

The tortillas and refried beans were given to the old man who passed them on to the sullen woman.

"Father Xhulin," began Mekel, "We've come to ask your advice, because I'm thinking of traveling to the finca in a few days to look for work. You who see everything and know everything by reading the days of Our Father God, what do you advise us?"

The man began to concentrate.

They glanced around the room in silence. There was a little

filthy-black table with a handful of red *tz'ite* beans, seeds of the tree used by their ancestors since ancient times. There was a hawk's foot, some string, and a bottle with yellowish liquid. On the mud walls hung a wide-eyed owl, and some heads of birds of prey. Lotaxh almost screamed when she turned her head and saw a dried snake right beside her face.

Xhulin asked the couple two or three questions, and then buried himself again in concentration.

He rolled up his pants and fixed his gaze on his naked leg, as he began a kind of monologue: "What is your will, O God of this world? Is it right that this son of yours should leave home to seek money in other lands or not?"

At that moment the heavy veins on his bare leg began to tremble, jumping convulsively in different places. Slapping his calf, the old man asked questions of the veins. If they moved, the answer was affirmative, if they stayed still, the answer was negative.

"Is it a good idea or not for Mekel to go to the finca?"

The veins jumped in three different places.

"Will his family have some misfortune while he is gone?"

No answer.

"Speak, tell me," he asked.

He took a handful of red *tz'ite* beans in his bony hands and threw them on the little table.

"Count them," he said to Lotaxh.

"I don't know how to count," she said.

"You count them," he said to Mekel. There were nineteen.

"Take them and throw them on the table," he told Mekel. He did as he was told. He counted them and this time there were twenty red beans. He did it again and there were twenty beans once more.

"Well," said the diviner, "I see a road going off into the distance that keeps getting smaller and smaller. There are a lot of people on it with heavy luggage. You're among those people," he told Mekel. "Many of the people, you included, aren't wearing a hat. Instead of gourds, others are carrying skulls on top of their suitcases or crates."

"A hat is a man's protection against the sun, and it is also an expression of his masculinity and safety. You should look for the protection of Our Father God and of the dear departed before starting your journey."

"And those that were carrying skulls instead of gourds, Father?" asked Lotaxh.

"Those are the ones who take their small children to the fincas and don't come back with them. They take them only to bury them. The sacred days order me to tell you that the trip will be successful. I see the work, I see the money that you can earn, but I also see the hot sun that will burn your head, and a foreman among the people with his whip. You must go and burn candles and incense to the cross, to the ancestors and to the mountain and the rocks to ask for protection. It should be on one of these days: Watan, Elab', Tox or B'en. Mother Nature, the burial grounds of our dead, and their spirits communicate and protect us mortals. Don't worry about your relatives; I can discern in the great work of the Spirit that there are no evil signs against your people. You can carry out your plans, trusting in the Great God," he concluded.

The couple busied themselves getting ready in the time remaining before Mekel's departure.

A few days later, a truck with a wooden railing was parked along with other trucks at the spot where the road ended in Jolomk'u.

At the crack of dawn a man honked his horn to let people know it was time to go, that their transportation was ready. It was the labor contractor, a man from the same community, but one who had acquired the ways of an exploiter of his own people.

Down the main trails shuffled men, women, children, and animals dragged by their owners. Each one clutched his or her miserable belongings stuffed inside a jute bag or crate. Each man carried a *cacaxte*, a kind of box bound together with sticks, and lined with a straw mat; inside was a change of ragged clothes, toasted corn, bags with herbal remedies for the children, refried beans for the road and perforated blankets. The crates had tools tied on top.

Everyone was carrying something; even the smallest children were used to carrying their own loads. The women had pots, griddles, plastic water pots, and gourds with water for the journey.

"It's getting late, hurry up," said the labor contractor.

Each man was followed by a woman; each woman had a group of children in tow on the rock-strewn trails; the children pulled their dogs and cats, chains of sad-faced families.

Some went to the fincas, others stayed to watch the truck until it disappeared.

Everyone wept, the travelers and those who stayed behind.

Among the last to arrive was a pregnant woman who hobbled up with a child in her arms and another clinging to her tattered skirt. She was leaving alone with her children, with her crate on her back.

It was past noon.

Lotaxh was among the women who had come to say good-bye to the men. She had made her husband some food for the trip: toasted corn, beans, and a jar of chile.

Many were drunk and waved good-bye lifting jars of liquor with corncob stoppers, the forlorn women filling them with tears.

As the people arrived, they adorned the old heap of a truck with their belongings. The railings were soon laden with gourds, pots, plastic containers, woven bags full of old things. Inside, the travelers settled down on some boards stretched the length of the truck. The children began to cry, even scream since it was so crowded. There were approximately a hundred people, including children and adults, pinned inside the rails, under the supervision of the labor contractor, who shouted orders with a barrage of insults.

The truck horn summoned the last travelers arriving late. Only a few of those on the contractor's list were still missing.

Soon a family appeared running down one of the mountain trails. The man forged ahead with a big box that he carried with a tumpline, signalling with his hand that they should wait for them. A woman came out of the underbrush with a load on her shoulder and a small child sitting on top of the load. The sandal of her left foot was broken and she carried it in her hand. She limped along over the stones. Last came a girl with uncombed hair and a dirty tear-stained face, with all her strength pulling at her dog, which was tied to the end of a rope.

The dog shook his head trying to free himself from bondage, as if to say: "No, don't take me." Just like the girl who was crying for her dog. The driver started the engine and honked for the last time. The girl's bundle fell from her shoulder, so now she struggled with the bag and the dog.

A young man went after her, as the truck began to roll, and the people began to settle down, with squeals of metal, wood, and human bones. They managed to lift up the young man and the child, but in the struggle she let go of the dog, which fell to the road, howling among the stones. It grew smaller and smaller in the tearful eyes of its owner, glued to the railing as the truck pulled away. That unfortunate dog was her sole possession.

The contractor looked in his dirty notebook and called out the names of those supposed to be going to work at the finca. Seventy-eight answered; two were missing.

"Those bastards are going to pay me back double," growled the man. "I even advanced them some of the money and now they don't show up."

"Attention everyone," he said. "We're not going to make any stops along the road. Don't make a nuisance of yourselves.

You can do your thing through the railings. It's late and we have to arrive at the finca tomorrow."

In the distance one could still hear the heart-rending cries of wives, children and parents who kept waving good-bye. Those going for the first time were frightened by the floor moving under their feet. They had never been in a motor vehicle, and they cried out on seeing the trees, mountains and hills moving and staying behind.

The truck was full of holes, rocks and dust. At every bump the boards on which the people sat lifted up. At first the jolts brought cries from the children and complaints from everyone. But little by little their bodies got used to the acute discomfort and they fell into a numbing stupor. They allowed themselves to be pulled along like abandoned objects. The children, attached to the breasts of their mothers, coughed and coughed, with their noses stopped up with dust and smoke. Drunken adults fell over and slept. Those who had been shouting or crying before were now hanging lifelessly between the boards of the pen. Their hats were anointed with pig, chicken and dog manure. They traveled forward and upward, reaching the high, rocky mountain range that resembled the spine of a bony horse.

Balancing like a parrot, Mekel clutched a corner of the pen, next to another man who had left his family. They travelled quietly as they climbed that range, the horizon extending and displaying itself before their eyes. They came to a place called Kab' Tz'in. It was a beautiful place. The hills rose out of an orange background of afternoon clouds below the dome of the sky. In the depths of the precipices ran tiny rivers that gnawed at the mountains. The road snaked around the hills, that dropped off precipitously into the depths until they became distant villages, spread out below. Immense rocks emerged beside ancient conifers covered with moss and ferns, smelling of old vegetation. The decaying underbrush gave off a lonely odor. Two of those rocks were Kab' Tz'in.

Solitary pines and cypresses were born, grew, and died, their crests covered with fog for most of the year. Kab' Tz'in: the two silent ones. It was the place where one could hear the silence of the centuries: a place of meditation to fill the spirit; a place of peace and tranquility for the soul.

The sun fell beyond the fiery horizon.

"One more day dies and one day less for us," said the man.

"And how many of us won't be coming back?" pondered Mekel, absorbed in his thoughts and in his sorrow.

A pack of wolves howled above the road among the rocks: terrifying howls of hungry beasts.

Almost no one noticed. The men slept as if drunk, the women with their children hanging on them nodded, grabbing the rails. The children, tired of crying, eased their discomfort by clinging to their mother's breasts.

The boards that served as seats were already falling apart under them. On the floor were chickens, cats and dogs, squashed and cold. Each family group rearranged itself, looking for a spot for their swollen rear ends. The stench became unbearable, the people were moved against their will by the jolts of the truck, heaving to the right and to the left. Human and animal waste, urine and vomit were everywhere.

The man who rode next to Mekel was much respected in the community. He had a lot of experience and knew the history of those places and those people. He was about seventy years old. Fate had led the two men toward the same destination.

"My father," began the man, "was named Paltol. He came through here many times under even worse conditions than those we're going through now. These roads hadn't even been built yet. There weren't any trucks like these. The trip was made on foot, or mule back. It took them three days to go from our town to the departmental capital."

"The authorities would often order them to get together to take sick people or loads too large for the animals. Once they ordered my father to carry a sick old man, a relative of one of the town officials. Because of his poor health, he couldn't ride a horse and had to be carried. One Sunday they found three young men to carry him, and one of them was my father. They were taken to the mayor, who told them to make enough tortillas and toasted corn cakes for a week-long trip to the city. They were to carry blankets and food and show up Tuesday morning at the house of a Ladino, Mr. Castañeda. There they would get their orders for the trip. The women worked all Monday at home preparing toasted corn cakes. As you know, tortillas go bad quickly, but toasted corn cakes are lighter, thanks to being toasted, and they last longer."

"On Tuesday only my father and another young man showed up. The third claimed he was sick. You can imagine, my friend, the trouble that young man had to go through. When they arrived at the Castañeda house they found everything ready for taking the ailing old man. There was a bundle of sleeping gear, food and a wooden chair fixed in such a way that it could be carried on a man's back. Another Ladino had a horse ready to go along with the sick man, and a pack mule to carry all of their luggage. They told the young men that they should take turns carrying the sick old man and that they should get to the city in no more than three days to see the doctor, because his health was very fragile. At first the journey went fairly quickly, but as time went on they got more and more tired and got only as far as Kab' Tz'in the first day. The sick man spent the whole time cursing them for any abrupt movement that bothered him."

"At the end of the first day they found a place to camp under a big outcropping, and they gathered enough firewood for the night, both to warm up the place and to frighten away the wild animals that roamed in those places, but the intense cold kept them from sleeping. The sick man spent the whole night complaining of his pains. The boys were used to discomfort and on account of their exhaustion, were able to sleep on their straw mats next to one another at the edge of the fire. At dawn the next day the Ladinos made their breakfast consisting of milk, coffee, meat, bread and eggs, which they carried in boxes and cans. The two young men filled their metal cups with toasted corn cakes and some hot coffee to soften them up. They had little corn tamales and some chile to finish off their breakfast."

"Before the sun came up on the trail, they had begun the trek with their backs sore from carrying the load. The man on horseback constantly cursed at the boys to make them pick up their pace."

"Each day they covered a shorter distance than the day before. After climbing the mountains, they crossed a number of rivers, ravines and rocky plains and went down countless hills until on the fourth day they managed to reach the city, faces covered with dried sweat, mixed with dust and salt. On their backs they had blisters and open sores. They carried their hard leather sandals together with their staffs. They could hardly bear the exhaustion that had overtaken their bodies."

"The patient didn't survive the operation the doctors performed on him. The boys went back alone with their bags."

"My father and my grandparents had to go through a lot of these experiences," the man went on. "There were those famous *mandamientos*, which consisted of constructing highways, bridges and buildings. Many people died from the forced labor."

"Those who didn't go to work outside the *municipio* had to work in Ladino homes fetching firewood, raising corn, or taking care of animals. The women had to wash clothes, do housework, make food for the workmen of ..." He was going to continue when a hard jolt interrupted him in the darkness.

The jolt brought desperate cries from children and adults. The people piled on top of one another at the front of the truck.

There was confusion everywhere as people sought one

another; children looking for parents and parents for children. Some wept; others cried out in terror; the rest tried to calm down the hysterical ones.

"What happened?" Mekel managed to ask as he was flung into the air.

"Calm down, calm down," shouted the contractor in the darkness. It's no big deal, the brakes just went out on the truck." The people didn't understand about brakes; all they knew was that they were sunk in darkness.

With the help of a flashlight they were able to see where the truck was stuck, and they could see that it had been stopped by a rock. Otherwise, they would have gone down a deep ravine.

It was eight o'clock at night, the cold was intense, and they were up close to 10,000 feet above sea level. The rush of the wind could be heard as it whistled through the pines. Gusts of drizzling rain beat against the trees sporadically; the clouds moved fast. They got out of the truck in the dark and looked for a place to hide from the rising wind and the rain. They drew close to one another behind a large boulder, sharing their misfortune. Some men managed to take the tarp off the truck and put it over the passengers. Later the full moon beamed a little light, enough for several men to go search for firewood and heat up some food for the complaining children. They made hot coffee with the remainder of the water that each one carried and spent the rest of the night huddled together under the same dark sky, under a cold country mist, in the middle of the darkness.

The next day the driver set about repairing the damage, a job that took all morning. But the provisions and the water became scarcer; there was nothing for making coffee. The merciless cold did not abate. The boys found some stagnate water nearby. Pushing aside the tadpoles and the leeches, they managed to fill two large earthen jars with a yellowish liquid, from which they made coffee for everyone. The food was pooled to give priority to the children, who were begging for tortillas. After midday, with everyone helping, they managed to free the truck, whose front hung over the ravine. They set it back up on the highway and the engine started. They felt relieved to leave that lonely and inhospitable place.

On approaching the first towns, they were ordered to spread the tarp over the overloaded truck to avoid problems at the police checkpoints. From there on they made the trip in the dark under the tarp, inhaling the exhaust fumes from the motor and the dust. Because of the lack of ventilation, the foul odors stopped up their lungs.

The children began to have difficulty breathing, some coughed, others complained of headaches, and the discomfort quickly spread because of the lack of oxygen. In desperation, the parents opened holes in different parts of the tarp and took turns breathing through them, until they arrived at the finca.

The majority arrived with various complaints: nausea, vomiting, diarrhea, headaches and sheer exhaustion. The next day, people were divided up for different activities: half went to the cotton plantations and the others to the coffee harvests.

Among the first enemies they had to contend with on arriving at the finca from the cold, high mountains, were the unbearable heat frying their bodies, causing them to sweat day and night and the swarms of mosquitoes, flies, gnats and other pests. The environment adversely affected their customs and way of life, food and dress. Their language could not be understood by the strangers among whom they worked, lived, and slept. Each group communicated in its own language. They were grouped separately according to region and could be distinguished by their languages, clothing and point of origin. There were speakers of Mam, K'iche', Tz'utujil, Q'anjob'al, Popti', Ixil and Kaqchikel. All children of the same father, all from the same roots: the Maya. Scattered, set loose, they wandered without a fixed destination after the catastrophe of the Spanish invasion. Their unity was shattered into a thousand pieces like clay pots smashed against the timeless rocks of social injustice. They now came together to share the same misfortune, brothers and sisters whom destiny had contrived to scatter in all directions. They arrived from different places like processions of ants, pushed by hunger, looking for an end to their misery.

Mekel had no experience in harvesting sugar cane, cotton or coffee, but he was there, he needed to do it, and he had to learn. He was among those slated to go to the cotton plantations.

"Is this the first time you've come to work here?" a man asked him.

"Yes sir."

"Do you know how to work cotton?"

"No, sir, I've never come here before."

"I work at a finca called *La Caldera*, and you?"

"They told me that I'm supposed to go to that same finca."

"I've been working here for two years. I'm from Sacapulas. At first it's real hard, buddy, but then your body either gets used to it or it dies. Nobody taught me the job; I learned from sheer tough luck and hard work. I had a real lousy foreman. Instead of a heart this guy had a stone, no feelings. He stole from you, insulted you, put you down constantly, and if he wanted to he'd even take your woman. He was worse than the owner of the finca. I'll tell you what you have to do. You have to get up real early because the sun is your worst enemy. La Caldera is an hour down the road. Those of us who work there leave at two in the morning and get the job done by eleven before the pot starts to boil."

"If you don't mind, I'd like to go with you, because I don't know the ropes," answered Mekel. "But sir, I need so much money for my place, that I wasn't planning to rest, but rather work all day."

"That's what we all say when we come the first time, full

of hope. You're not going to become one of the rich folks in this place—those spots are already taken. If you manage to gather eighty pounds of cotton, minus what the foremen deduct, you have to consider yourself lucky. What I'd advise you is to take a gallon of water or a gourd. Those first days you get real thirsty, and the water there isn't too good. Which shack are you in?"

"No. 20," said Mekel.

"When you hear the whistle, come with us. We're the first ones out."

"Great, thanks a lot."

Under the light of the full moon bathing the landscape, Mekel's eyes reviewed the great expanse stretching all the way to infinity. He was astonished. It looked like an infinite blanket of kernels of white corn covering the earth. The soft ocean breeze that arose at this hour was fresh. The work began. Each one took over his own furrow; the rest advanced quickly. Mekel, with his hands used to a different kind of labor, struggled clumsily in the tangle of the shrubs.

"Don't worry, that's the way we all do at first," they encouraged him. He wasn't hungry, just very, very thirsty.

By ten o'clock the chubby gourd with the waist of a pretty girl was empty.

"You better eat some corn, my friend," someone advised, "because lots of water can hurt you. Lots of guys have gotten bloated from drinking too much water. It's not good for you. And the worst part is that you can get malaria."

At noon the sun's rays fell in a vertical line, roasting the backs of the men who still remained at work. The rest slept stretched out under the shade of the quiet leafy trees, with their hats over their faces. The leaves were motionless, not stirred by even a hint of air, as though nature was now holding her breath. There was a suffocating quiet. The gnats were buzzing. Clothing stuck to the workers' bodies. Mekel wanted to keep working, but that oven clouded over his senses and he was satisfied with half a load. He went to rest in the shade just like the others.

When he went back that afternoon, he was carrying the tortillas the corn-grinding woman had put in his bag. His mouth was dry, his face chalky from the salt that had dried with his sweat.

Shack No. 20, like all the rest, was open on the sides, an open-air barracks with a roof of palm leaves.

Each family group laid out its own territory in that strange place under the communal roofs. The first few nights, Mekel couldn't fall asleep. He tossed and turned on the hard mat, and when he was about to doze off, the mosquitoes came humming in his ears and bit him on his face, arms, legs, everywhere. Slaps here, scratches there and more sweaty twists and turns until he surrendered to exhaustion, giving up the fight and remaining at the mercy of mosquitoes, fleas, lice and other pests, the enemies of those piled-up people.

Because the heat was unbearable, nobody put on their blankets, or even lay on top of them. After midnight the heat would abate and that was when the snoring began, providing an opportunity for the parasites to gorge on blood or inject their poison, which sooner or later manifested itself in the form of various diseases.

It often happened that someone would come down with shaking, chills, fever, and jaundiced faces. It was a sign that they carried malaria germs, which meant loss of work, and strength and finally, death. Sometimes, with luck, quinine managed to cure them in time, but most people, particularly children, died in a few weeks. One of those nights when Mekel couldn't fall asleep, he heard someone moaning, and got up to help him. It was an old man who twisted and turned because of illness. Someone said that there was a healer in the neighboring barracks, and he went looking for him with his flashlight. It made his flesh creep to see half-naked women, men and children completely covered with mosquitoes buzzing in a funereal chorus. One boy, who was passing his hand over his face, was awakened by the flashlight, and Mekel asked where the healer was. The boy pointed to where the man was.

"Please come see him," Mekel begged.

"Don't worry, my friend. It's malaria, just give him some quinine. There are lots of people with that disease, and if I made a point of visiting each of them, I wouldn't sleep all night. Give him quinine, enough quinine," and he turned over to go back to sleep.

During Mekel's first month at the finca, more than ten adults and children died from various diseases: malaria, parasites, malnutrition, while others died of poisoning from the constant crop spraying and a few from alcoholism.

At night Mekel spent a long time thinking about his family, about Lotaxh, about little Lwin, who was growing more each day. He thought also of those children with whom he shared a roof.

The first month had gone by and the next day, Saturday, was pay day. He was looking forward to getting the money for the month's work, which he calculated to be thirty-six loads of cotton. He was getting used to the work and hoped to up his goal for the next month. In his mind he fondled this money, which he would send along with someone going back to Jolomk'u, so he could start paying off his debt and help out Lotaxh.

Saturday there were long lines at the finca's administrative offices. The foremen, armed to the teeth, kept order, shouted, insulted, threatened and used their night sticks to impose order. The submissive people, without saying a word, waited their turn under the burning sun. They kept their ears tuned to hear their names called, otherwise they would be left until last. When they were called they answered loudly.

"Martín Pascual!"

"Here!"

"You get paid for twenty loads. It's not much. You've been working six months and you're still not doing any better. Turn in more or go to hell, because we don't need any lazy slobs around here."

"Very good, sir."

He swallowed his humiliation into the depths of his soul, without being able to externalize it. To avoid problems he had to accept what they paid, without protest, without grimacing, but with humility and simplicity. These were the marks of a good worker.

"Antonio Mateo!"

"Here!"

"You did thirty-five loads. But here is the list of what you got from the pharmacy, the store, the bar and the tools you were given. Deducting all of that, you get ten quetzales and eighty centavos."

"Sir, the pharmacy and the store are correct, but the bar and the tools aren't. I didn't drink this month, since my kids are sick."

"No son, nobody's trying to cheat you. You must have gotten so soused that you didn't remember buying booze and other stuff. Get back, I've got work to do."

"Sorry, sir."

The food ration, consisting of scant corn and beans given out each week, was deducted from the pay of those who, according to the records of the administrator and the foremen, had not done an acceptable amount of work.

They were half way through the list, when the man called:

"Miguel Pedro!"

"Here!"

"Twenty for you."

"Sir," he said, his voice trembling. "According to my calculation I did thirty-six bales of cotton."

"That's your calculation, but you Indians don't know how to count, nor is it worth teaching you. The report I have here says that it's twenty."

"But sir, that's not fair. I did over a bale daily after the first three days."

"You're new here, right?"

"Yes, sir."

"I don't think you really need the money too badly. Go to the end of the line and we'll talk about it when I finish my work. Next!" said the paymaster, irritated by Mekel's boldness.

One of the armed guards came up to the paymaster, and they talked quietly for a minute. Then one of the gunmen addressed the gathering: "If anyone isn't satisfied with his pay, he can go to the end of the line and there will be time to settle his case," pointing at the endless line of people.

After that nobody even thought of protesting or voicing any disagreement.

It was past noon. Those who already knew the ropes carried tortillas, but the newcomers had not, and were hungry. When it was Mekel's turn, they had already turned on the electric light at the finca.

"You're the dissatisfied one, are you?," asked the paymaster.

He didn't answer.

"I want you to tell me where you learned those stupid ideas of 'justice' and 'rights'. Who taught them to you?"

He remained silent.

"Don't come to me with such foolishness. We don't want people to come and put these dumb ideas in the heads of our good workers, who are peaceful and respectful. If it wasn't for the work that we give you here in the finca, you Indians would keep on eating garbage back home." Saying this, he threw some bills on the table.

Mekel took them and left hat in hand.

The next week he worked with a foreman who kept an eye on him. He was given a special task, working in a spot where there was a limited amount of second-rate cotton, so he'd have a harder time picking a bale. This caused a noticeable drop in his income.

As time went by, Mekel had a variety of experiences, getting to know other people and trying to help those who needed him.

Five long months had gone by since he left Jolomk'u. On two occasions he had sent money to Lotaxh, not as much as he would have liked, but enough so they wouldn't have too much trouble at home. He had received two packages from Lotaxh brought by villagers who had come down to the finca. He was told that everyone was fine and that little Lwin was growing every day; that he was crawling around on the mats beside his working mother.

Sometimes he felt like leaving it all and returning to his village, to his people, and stop being just a faceless worker. His labor was all that mattered in the cauldron of the finca.

One hot afternoon when the sun was forming mirages on the fiery ground, his eyes clouded over, his ears began to buzz, and he felt a headache coming on. He stopped working and looked for the shade of a ceiba tree. He sweated profusely even in the shade. He imagined that the infinite blue vault was a large sweat bath. The expanse of sky was cloudless. He laid his hat to one side, and before him on a rock, a lizard looked up to the sky and breathed with its mouth desperately open. Seated in the shade on the dried-up leaves, he had time to think about those far away. He returned to Jolomk'u, thought of each of his loved ones, and promised himself never to return to this hellish climate. He traced imaginary lines in his mind, comparing his life there with how he lived on the finca. He stretched out on the dry leaves and fell into a deep sleep with his hat over his face.

When he woke up, the sun was peeking at him through the leaves of the ceiba, and the afternoon was getting cooler. He looked in his bag for something to eat, but it was full of the ants that had chewed holes in the tortillas. He shook out the napkin, took one last swallow of warm water from the bottom of his gourd and returned to the hut.

In Jolomk'u things were getting worse by the day. Hunger afflicted those families whose granaries were already empty. There were no ears of corn in the attics, and the corn was just beginning to sprout. It would be five more months until the next harvest.

More truckloads of workers came down to the fincas. The rate of pay went down, because labor was abundant. The villages were becoming empty. The consumption of corn was rationed, and they supplemented their diets with the wild plants people found in the mountains.

Lotaxh's granary still had enough corn for about two more months, and then she would have to start buying some. She had gotten money twice, but she didn't want to use it. She wanted to repay the loan as soon as possible. She had managed to save some money from the sale of the eggs her hens laid. The pigs were fattened and sold, and she made clay pots and griddles in her free time or at night when her son was asleep. Her savings were piling up in the little gourd where she kept them. She spent only what was absolutely necessary for her child. She tried to save every penny that came into her hands.

Several months went by without anyone from Jolomk'u going to the finca where Mekel was working. Most people went to other fincas, attracted by the sugar cane or coffee harvest. Cotton work held no attraction for them. All these months she received no news from Lwin's father. Then one day the boy who had brought the money from Mekel the second time said he was going back for a few more months. He was planning to get married and needed some money.

Lotaxh was greatly relieved to know the boy was going, and she ran to look for the scribe, but he was not there. He had left the village for a few days.

Only two days were left until the boy was to make the trip.

She felt the urgency of sending a letter to Mekel, letting him know how the family was. When she couldn't find the scribe, Lotaxh decided to go to a Ladina woman she knew in town, doña Licha, to ask her to write the letter. Doña Licha was a lady who gave shots, prescribed medicines, cured children of the evil eye, and did favors for less money than the rest of the Ladinos. But the main thing people looked her up for was for writing letters, because she could speak their language, as long as it wasn't in front of any other Ladinos. God forbid that a Ladino should relate socially with Mayas, never. To protect herself from the "what will people say?" of the others, doña Licha took her clients to a room at the back of her house. This is what she did when she wrote Lotaxh's letter.

"Dear Mekel," she began, "everybody in the family is all right by the grace of God. I got what you sent both times: the first with don Marcos and the other with José, who is now going back there. Lwin is fine now, although he got sick three times: the first time he couldn't breathe because his soft spot fell in; the second time, from the evil eye, because your father came to visit the house when he was hot blooded; and the third time my milk was cold, because I got wet; but among us all, we made him get well. Don't worry about the corn, we're buying some and will have enough."

"I've finished weeding the cornfield, and I'm taking care of the animals like you said."

"Take care of yourself and I hope you come back soon."

"I'm sending you a few things and I hope they arrive okay. All the family is well, except for your brother Antonio, who is suffering from a curse. The diviner says that they put frogs in his stomach, and now they are curing him with some remedies; only the diviner knows what they are."

"It won't be long before there's new corn. The cornfield is fine."

"Take good care of yourself, because your mother is having lots of bad dreams with coffins in them. The dogs are barking all night; they must be seeing something."

"Don't worry about us. Good-bye."

Lotaxh would have liked to be more explicit in her letter, but because she was dealing with strangers, she included only what was most necessary. She didn't say she had received money, because this was something she didn't want doña Licha to know. She would have liked to find someone she trusted or to be able to write herself, but she could not.

Folding the sheet, she put it in an envelope with the name "Miguel Pedro" on it and then gave it to Lotaxh.

"Thanks so much, doña Licha. How much do I owe you for this big favor?" she asked in her own language.

"Three quetzales, dear. But if you don't have the cash, you can bring me a chicken on Sunday."

"Here they are," she said.

Lotaxh took advantage of her trip to town to buy five ten-centavo rolls, a pound of mutton, two pounds of brown sugar, and some other things that she sent along with the boy, who would travel the next day to the finca.

Mekel received the letter several weeks late, because he had left and was already working at another finca.

●●●●

Life in Jolomk'u was very difficult for those who lived there. It was no different for Lotaxh, although with her tenacity for work, she was getting ahead in the struggle to survive. She brought one of her ten brothers and sisters to live with her, partly to lighten the financial burden on her father and partly to have some company in the absence of her husband. The girl, who was ten years old, helped with the housework and the care of little Lwin, whom she carried everywhere.

One day after she had finished her work in the cornfield, Lotaxh took stock of her contributions to the family's support, and figured that since Mekel left she had fattened three pigs, which were sold at a good price, five more kids had been born, and her three hens had livened up the courtyard with twenty-five yellow chicks. She had gone without a lot of things. Twice a week she fed her son an egg and she slaughtered a hen every two or three months. Most of the time she was satisfied with her tortillas and her wild vegetables, beans and chile. She tried to find the most tender parts of water cress and nightshade, as well as tendrils of the chayote squash, all of which were very good for nursing mothers.

The savings from the egg sales grew in the broken pot. There was a different hiding place for the profits made from selling pots. She calculated the total without knowing how to count. The money sent by Mekel, added to what lay at the bottom of her little gourd, was enough to pay off her husband's loan, but she didn't want to do it until he was there. He would arrive soon, any time now. Every afternoon after the daily bus arrived she would go out to see if he was on it. She imagined seeing him arrive with his trunk on his shoulder full of surprises, like the others returning from the finca, bringing back ephemeral pleasures.

This year the work in the fields had been Lotaxh's responsibility. To avoid having to pay a day laborer, she had worked the land herself. With the hoe she turned over the soil; she planted the corn, and did the first and second weedings. Wherever she went she took her small child and left him under the shade of the tree, one eye on her work and the other on Lwin.

Each corn plant was a handful of hope that grew. They were green illusions whose tops signalled to the blue sky over the woman's head. She dreamed that one day her children would live without the misery and deprivation she was going through. Her hands were covered with calluses, her feet were split by the earth and she healed them at night with hot lard. Her shoulders, peering out between the shreds of coarse cloth, were toasted by the sun.

No, they should not suffer this way.

"But how can it be?'" she asked herself. "If we Maya are born to suffer," replied a voice inside of her, "that is our destiny."

Before returning to her hovel, she would sit for a moment on a stone to nurse her child:

"Hurry my child, because it's getting late. Maybe your father is already waiting at home," she said to herself. She spoke so as not to feel lonely, to teach her son to speak, or maybe to keep her hopes up and fill the emptiness in her soul.

If she wasn't too tired out from the day's work, she would cut firewood and carry it on her shoulders, the hoe on top of her load and her son bundled in a sheet hanging from her neck. All of life was a rush; one was always rushing.

"Some day, my son, we'll buy a beast of burden so we won't have to carry firewood on our backs" she told him. "When you're big you'll cut wood and you'll tie it on the animal with a leather strap or rope and you'll put your hoe on top. That way your back won't hurt and the sticks won't poke your ribs; your hair will grow everywhere without a bald spot worn by the tumpline."

When she got home, she left the child with her sister, who had already prepared the tortilla dough. She lifted her clay pot to her shoulder, the colander for draining the corn in one hand and another container in the other, and went to the spring. When she returned, she picked up the grinding stone to start smashing the corn. She made the tortillas, fed the animals, washed diapers: thus ended her days, one after another.

On one of the house posts she marked each full moon that passed since he had left. The marks were wounds on the barkless post, replicas of the woman's internal wounds.

In three days it would be market day. She hadn't been to town for several weeks, but this time she would go.

There were various griddles, pots, pitchers, all of fired clay; she would take them to market to sell. She also tied two fat chickens, carefully wrapped up a dozen eggs, and on the afternoon before she collected handfuls of wild greens from her land to add to her merchandise. She had arranged ahead of time with a neighbor to lend her his mule to carry the goods.

It took her two hours to cover the distance between Jolomk'u and the town. She made her way down the road and greeted people along the way. The mule went ahead, attached to the end of the rope with the pots, griddles, greens and chickens. They quickly found a good spot among the merchants in the plaza.

From every place, down all the roads, from the villages came the people in black and white *güipiles* and *capixayes* woven by their own hands. They were in uniform, like Maya everywhere, for whatever ancient reason. They themselves knew not why.

The blue day extended over the plaza; it was the communal square, situated in front of the church and the town offices, on the naked earth where the people of the region congregated. Market day was the appropriate day for commercial, social, and spiritual exchange. It was a place where everything was talked about, where people looked for each other after long absence. They had been immersed in their own problems, but now they showed up, saying "Hey, we're still here!" A place where they sold salt (the kind that gives you goiter), corn for times of hunger, crude brown sugar to sweeten the Sunday coffee and, if there were enough centavos, a pound of meat.

The rays of sunshine found Lotaxh settled in a good spot surrounded by her merchandise, and facing the crowds. She showed her wares to potential buyers. The chickens were on the ground and when people asked about them, Lotaxh let them pick them up by their feet. People were arriving with boxes, trunks, and bundles. There was a little of everything: quick lime in lumps, loads of pitch pine, boxes of *xheka* buns, string bags made from black wool, white wool, fruit, vegetables, tables with colored soda pop in glass bottles, and many people.

There was a crowd of people. Lotaxh's sister's heart sank when she saw so many people for the first time. The people were noisy, the animals were noisy, everyone was noisy; one had to shout to be heard.

When morning High Mass, unattended by Ladinos, was over, out poured the Maya jostling one another. Outside it was cold, but they came out sweating. As they emerged they spilled out into the streets and to the market to make their purchases for the week. In this first wave of people, bunches of vegetables were sold and some people bought breakfast after mass. Some earthenware was sold and Lotaxh got orders for two weeks hence.

The chickens, some eggs and griddles remained. The Ladinos would come; they get up later, she thought, glancing up at the sun and noticing that it was still early.

The eggs were sold as well as the griddles, but the chickens were still there on the ground.

A long time went by and a Ladina woman came by, bringing a Mayan girl with two heavy baskets half full of all kinds of groceries. She looked at Lotaxh and said:

"How much are you asking for these skinny chickens, honey?"

She shook her head and told the girl that she didn't understand.

"Señorita Amarilis, she says that she doesn't understand Spanish."

"You ask her then."

Upon being asked by the interpreter, Lotaxh said in her limited Spanish:

"Three quetzales, ma'am."

"For these weightless things! That's robbery, you know. How dare you! It's against the law. It's not allowed, honey, it's not allowed. Right now you could go to jail. Here comes a policeman who could take you in for overcharging. The most your chickens are worth would be one quetzal each. You can't steal, honey, it's a sin and God punishes that. These animals just grow up on their own eating grass, you don't have to spend anything to raise them." Having said this, she stuffed the birds into her basket.

Lotaxh didn't understand a single word, but from the lady's gestures she could tell that she was upset.

"Take the money, because if you don't, she says she'll put you in jail," the girl translated. "She's a friend of the mayor."

Amarilis was used to using threats and humiliation to get her way. The sense of superiority had deeper roots in that woman than in the rest of the Ladinos. Nevertheless, she was the first to carry Our Lady of Sorrows on her shoulders in the

Holy Week processions, and bought the new clothes for the Patron Saint for the town fiesta.

After that humiliation Lotaxh put away the two quetzales. As she watched her chickens go off in the basket, she cried inside, whether from rage or sorrow, she wasn't sure.

"You can't argue with Ladinos," advised her companion, "especially now that Mekel isn't here. It's better not to have anything to do with them."

The other vendors nearby had left, covering up their wares when they saw that woman coming, to avoid being her victims. A tax collector came by and greeted Amarilis, doffing his hat.

Lotaxh couldn't buy much of what she had planned to get because of the low price for the chickens. She only bought what was necessary.

When she got up from the plaza, it was almost noon, and it was hot. She bought rice cooked in milk for her sister and her son and a fruit drink for herself before they returned to Jolomk'u.

Hunger continued to scourge the region. Children and adults were emaciated and did not have the strength to work. People went farther and farther to look for food. The men went out to hunt spotted cavies, armadillos and wildfowl with their blow guns and slingshots. Death began to ride inside boxes of all sizes, followed by funeral processions dressed in white, mainly women. The men had dispersed in all directions to search for sustenance. More and more people died of hunger.

"Today about fifteen dead people were taken to the cemetery," said the *ajtz'ib'*, when he came back from town. "They are coming from all the villages. Those who don't find people to carry them are burying them right there, since most of the men have gone to the finca. There's not much work there either. Many are coming back after having looked in vain. They say there are too many laborers coming from other towns and they're not paying very much."

The days, weeks and months went. Thirteen Ajaw was coming around again, the third and last celebration for Lwin. But in Jolomk'u nobody was thinking about festivities. People were looking for corn. The trucks arriving with corn from other places were awaited anxiously, and they sold only one measure to each family who came to the town hall. After the long line of Ladinos, the Maya followed in interminable lines, only to return to their villages with empty sacks.

At Lotaxh's they celebrated Thirteen Winaq, which was the conclusion of the *tzolkin*, or calendar round, consisting of thirteen calendar cycles since the birth of Lwin. On account of the scarcity of food, there were few chickens, but Lotaxh butchered two of them in order to be able to invite the closest relatives and the godparents. The event passed almost unnoticed. There were no fireworks to awaken the mountains, nor bearers of food for the godparents. They talked of nothing but hunger and death.

"Soon it will be our turn," said the godmother, filling her bowl with chicken soup for the second time. She was talking about death. "Three of my grandchildren," she went on, "are sick in bed. They've lost their appetite and all they want to do is sleep. The fox comes and howls night after night near the house. The owl is hooting nearby. That's what happened when the late Xhapin died: the animals howled every night until she died."

"Here's the little lamb," said Lwin's grandfather, as he handed the child to the godfather, who had a pair of scissors in his hand. He had gone to fetch him where he was playing with the other small children.

"Thank you," answered the godfather. He took the child in his arms and played with him for a while, and then he said:

"In the name of Ajaw, who is present at this ceremony, I hereby cut this lock of hair as a symbol that you have reached the age of becoming a member of the community. The first shearing of a little lamb takes place when it can walk alone, and becomes independent of the mother's care. So also with a person, who upon reaching this age, completes the first stage of his existence. May God keep you and watch over you, and over this lock of your hair, which will be saved in a little bag and kept until the day of your death. It will be put in your coffin to accompany you on the search for Ajaw, your protector in the next life," said the godfather. He gave the lock of hair and the candle to the godmother, and she placed it at the bottom of the chest.

Old Lwin, for whom the baby was named, took the child and speaking for everyone began:

"By the will of the Great Spirit, who is manifested in the sun, the moon, the stars, the mountains, rivers, air and water, you have lived these two hundred and sixty days. We give thanks to he who rules over the day and the night, the maker of the universe." Then he put a small *capixay* on him and continued, "You will take care to perpetuate our names and honor the memory of the ancestors who founded our race, by practicing our eternal values."

The child began to cry upon feeling himself suspended in air.

Among the guests was a couple who a few days before had returned from the fincas carrying the third letter from Mekel. There was great interest in knowing how things were going. After the little ceremony someone asked after the father of the child.

"At first the climate was really hard on him," said the woman. "He was sick and we took care of him for several days. He worked too hard."

"You can't imagine how many problems one runs into there," continued the husband, "especially when you go there for the first time. You arrive full of hope and wanting to work as much as you can, but a lot of things keep you from doing so: the change of climate, the bugs, the contaminated water, the poor housing and our customs. But the worst enemy of all is the men that take advantage of us. All of them: the labor contractor, the foreman, the administrator, and the owners take advantage of us. Values like cooperation, respect, and solidarity are easily lost. In their place appear egotism and the hatred of others, because one learns to serve only one's own interest, when you see so much injustice. People aren't valued there, just their work."

"We women don't have a sweat bath for bathing like we do here," the wife noted, "so we have to go down to the river or among the coffee trees where others spy on us openly. Many girls have been raped by unscrupulous men with the consent and complicity of the local authorities. They don't respect our customs."

"Now that we've come back," continued the woman, "Mekel has to fix his own food and wash his own clothes, which we took care of up until we left."

Lotaxh's heart swung back and forth between sorrow and nostalgia. Her mother-in-law, Mekel's mother, came up to offer her liquor that so far had been served only to the men. "Drink it, honey," she said, "Your sorrow can only be drowned with this, with a drink." She indicated how much with her dirty fingernail and raised the bottle to Lotaxh's mouth. She needed it.

A little later the women weeped loudly on the small mats next to their husbands.

"Forgive us, friends, that we haven't been able to treat you the way we would like to, but you know our situation. Take a little corn, you can eat it at your place," said Lotaxh.

"Thank you," said the godfather, "you shouldn't have bothered. You're alone and in this time of scarcity without your husband, you've really done a lot. Forgive us for coming with empty hands. We're going through one of the worst times in the history of our people."

After this last gathering in Lwin's honor, Lotaxh devoted herself to caring for the cornfield and the housework, alternating it with pottery making and weaving. On rainy days when she couldn't go to weed the cornfield, she made pots or clothing to sell. Her son was her constant companion. Wherever she went, the child went on her back, sometimes asleep and sometimes wide awake. She was accustomed to talking to her little son in the loneliness of the fields, where the leaves of the corn plants were turning green and multitudes of multicolored birds took shelter. She cut wild flowers and gave them to the child.

"Listen, son," she said. "listen to the song of the birds. Learn to hear the silence and the language of nature. It's beautiful." They stayed a long time in harmonious silence, and then the concert of the birds began, the murmur of elongated leaves, the birth of green lakes of corn, the eternal flow of abundant rivers that scattered foam in their descent. Mother and child gazed into one another's eyes in silence. Suddenly, he cried out. The silence was broken by Lwin's voice, harmonizing with the other sounds, animating the silence.

Lotaxh surveyed her fields in order to be able to inform Mekel as soon as he arrived. She looked over the furrows, the stalks of plants, dreaming of ears of corn full of yellow grain. She pulled out the weeds growing among the plants. She squashed the fleeing beetle larvae and cut up the earthworms into little pieces. Her eyes followed the bees and butterflies, taking turns at each flower. She walked among the furrows, which were like half-lit alleys, covering up the entrances to the moles' burrows, destroying their nests to keep them from multiplying and damaging her plants.

The sun set through a gap in the clouds, scratching the sky with a handful of rays, and tracing a rainbow on the distant landscape.

"This is the bottle-gourd flower," she said. "It's yellow and represents our happiness. This is the bell flower. It's purple and is the color of the Great Spirit, the color of his dwelling place and of the world that remains beyond death. This is the color red, which we carry in our veins, it's the name of that which is beautiful and pleasant to our eyes, and forms part of our existence. Take it."

The child held flowers of different colors and smells in both hands. The rainbow was fading away with the afternoon. She washed her feet in the winding brook, scrubbing them against the pumice stone. She did it to feel part of the dying afternoon more than anything else. It was satisfying to feel the water and the air; all of her senses were suffused with nature's bounty. A painful nostalgia for beauty transported her beyond the material world. It didn't happen often, but this afternoon she felt like crying and laughing at the same time, like flying through the air.

But it was growing late. It was time to leave everything the way it was and to look for shelter in her little home.

"Chiwit, chiwit," she called the dog working hard at chasing butterflies and dragonflies, or looking for rodents in their burrows. The dog barked in the distant cornfield.

"Agú, agú," said Lwin and then became quiet and motionless. When the dog barked closer by, the baby began to wiggle on his mother's back. And when the lame dog came up to them, the little one jumped and laughed and moved from one side to the other. As Lotaxh walked home, the child slept until he was put to bed back home.

There was no harvesting done at the finca on Sundays. The men went to town to buy what they needed for the week, to rest a while under the ceiba tree in the town park, and to chat with their friends.

The women stayed in the shelters and aired the blankets to kill the lice and fleas that abounded in their clothes. Others went to the river to wash their clothing, their children and themselves with a black soap that stripped the dandruff off their rough scalps. On Sunday afternoons they would mend their clothes under the shade of the trees, half-humming folk tunes under their breath. Perhaps they remembered their families and the village hut so far away. The children played on the dusty earth, chasing one another, smudge-faced, half-naked urchins under the banana and sapote trees near their communal barracks.

One Sunday, Mekel agreed to go along with some of his fellow workers who lived under the same roof. He had washed his clothes the day before, and he wanted to buy some things in town and enjoy the company of his friends. They would have a chance to run into people they knew in that sultry town and trade news about their home towns. Mekel learned that corn was expensive at home and that people were dying of hunger. This news brought to mind the image of his little Lwin.

"You know what people are doing back home?" asked the man with the news. "Since the corn hasn't ripened and the new corn is barely starting, the people grind it cob and all and make it into gruel. The animals have been sold, the people are up in the mountains looking for edible greens and sick people shut themselves up to wait for death with their children in the solitude of their homes. The corn that comes in from time to time isn't enough for all the people arriving from all of the hamlets."

The men had nothing to nourish their conversation under the great ceiba, in the midst of the tobacco smoke

One of the friends suggested they escape the heat in the shade of some bar with a few cold beers. On Sunday their throats deserved something cold. Everyone agreed, with the exception of Mekel, who argued that he needed to visit other people from his town and go back and wash his clothes. But the real reason for his refusal was that he didn't want to use any of his savings. The others insisted, so he agreed to go for a little while in order to placate them.

The inside of the bar reeked of fermented *chicha*. The phonograph was going full blast with *ranchera* music, getting the men all stirred up. It looked like another cotton field with all the white Mexican-style Sunday hats filling the rooms and hall, surrounding rustic tables full of dark bottles. Everyone had a curved machete on his waist. The new arrivals sat in a corner at a table with four wooden benches.

"What will you have?" asked a pale woman with a bright red mouth.

"Four ice-cold beers," answered one of the men.

"Just three beers, and one soda," corrected Mekel.

"But the soda costs the same as the beers," explained the waitress.

"It doesn't matter," answered Mekel.

The rest didn't like that, but they accepted grudgingly. Someone chose a piece on the nickelodeon. The invisible keys of a marimba sent a melody through the air and linked the men together in remembrance of the world they had left behind.

Mekel noticed from his corner how the ambiance quickly transformed those men. It was a place sown with illusions, where men went in search of relief and came out defeated. They looked for refuge from their troubles, but their disappointment multiplied and became a heavier burden. From a distance, everything looked attractive: liquor, women, music, laughter, and gaiety. But in reality they went there to deposit the result of all their sweat and sacrifice in the fields. Most of those who went in left with empty pockets, leaving their Sunday hats pawned and their curved machetes piled up.

Mekel could watch the whole festive scene and the

progressive effect of the drinks on the customers' spirits. One woman who looked like an immense blob of gelatin, was the cashier. She told the rest of the faded girls with red lips what to do: "Kick out that drunk, serve the men at that table; take some more fried pork rinds over there; pick up the glasses; change the music; wait on those men ..." From her high stool she surveyed her domain, fleecing the unlucky ones who ventured inside the saloon.

"What does it say on those signs hanging on the wall?" Mekel asked the friend beside him. The other read the poster: "If you come here to drink to forget your troubles, you better pay before you drink, so you won't forget to pay."

It was the first time Mekel had visited one of those places. He was so possessive of the *centavos* he had managed to scrape together that he didn't spend them on unnecessary things. This was a new experience for him, and it made him sad to see how easily the bills came out of the men's pockets, knowing that many of the children and relatives of those carefree tipplers were dying of hunger.

The men revealed a range of emotions: some chattered merrily in between gales of laughter; others conversed with respect and courtesy; some sobbed and consoled one another; others farther off argued passionately at the top of their voices. Some were out cold and were sleeping it off on the rustic tables or lay in the sawdust scattered on the floor, only to be dragged out by the women, who made them the laughing stock of the place. They were stretched out one on top of another on the sidewalk in front of the bar with their pockets hanging out like deflated balloons. They had vomited and urinated on themselves, and were practically unconscious.

"Don't drink anymore, it's getting late. Let's go back," Mekel pleaded with his friends, who were starting to raise their voices.

"What do you want us to do?" one of them interrupted. "What else can I do except get drunk to forget all the suffering and pain I'm carrying here inside. I'm like that volcano you see over there. I'm trying to relieve my grief and sorrow. I know this isn't the best way to resolve my problems, but it's the only way I can speak up and share this moment with you. You listen and understand me because we have had the same experiences. You're something to hold onto, and I'm reaching out to you to keep afloat and avoid being shipwrecked. You give meaning to my existence, because even I myself forget I exist."

Petlon, the woman who provided Mekel his meals in his new job, had come a few months before to the finca with her whole family. She had seven children. The oldest was twelve and went with the father to pick cotton. The ten year old girl helped her mother prepare food for the twenty men for whom she was responsible. Petlon hardly had time to sleep, with so much work to do: she got up before the men went out to the fields, and she went to bed after everyone else was asleep. Every day she had to cook the corn, wash the cooked grain, grind and make tortillas, cook the pot of beans and the corn gruel for the field hands. Father and mother worked ceaselessly to care for their little children as far as their strength allowed. In spite of everything, in spite of their intense struggle, they watched sadly as the health of the little ones deteriorated. Four of them had pale sad little faces and stomachs swollen so much that they could not see their own feet. They were drowsy day and night. They slept with goose bumps on their skin, like cold little chickens snuggled up against each other. They didn't eat their tortillas nor drink their corn gruel. They just slept or cried all the time. The *curanderos* said it was *susto* that drained the blood from their faces. Others said that maybe their *nawales* had gotten lost on the road to the finca. They needed to call them to the bank of the river with a water pot. There were some who thought they might have worms and that there was nothing better than garlic and chenopodium seeds crushed, wrapped in newspaper and tied on their stomachs for three consecutive days. The docile mother tried everything the neighbors, friends and healers suggested, but the children just kept on getting worse.

One morning, stealing a moment from her pile of work, Petlon took four of the children, two boys and two girls, to the edge of the great river that tumbled down over the rocks, leaving the coffee and banana trees behind on its way toward the ocean. She set the four of them on a griddle-like rock surrounded by foam. She gave them white flowers to take apart and had them throw the petals one by one into the river. The petals separated like aimless canoes on the small waves. Next she passed eggs over their bodies, from head to foot. They were eggs from the chickens, that were then broken against the rocks. The mother chewed rue with water, and rubbed their faces vigorously without warning. It took their breath away and they sighed deeply. This was the way you cured them of the evil eye and of *susto*. The children kept throwing into the river the white petals that dodged the rocks on their way to the sea.

Is this the way innocent souls were sent to the sea of eternity without having had the opportunity to enjoy life on earth? Was this how the curve on statistical charts snaked ever upward to mark the high rate of mortality and morbidity that were part of this beautiful Mayan land, becoming one of the highest in the world? In this fleeting existence, hundreds of thousands of sad faces and swollen bellies fall like stars in the dark night of social injustice.

The children's tear glands had already dried up and they sobbed without tears. The parents and everyone else nearby had become used to their moaning. People hardly noticed them any more, since they were part of the monotonous noise of the workers' barracks. But finally they got so tired of being kept awake that one Sunday they decided to build a hut out of palm leaves for the family in an isolated place among the coffee trees. The mother had spent several sleepless nights, and the circles under her eyes were like black clouds. The others tried to give her support and comfort her. The money she got every two weeks from grinding corn was spent on medicine and treatments. But to no avail.

"How are the children doing?" asked the father upon returning from work.

"Three of them are the same. The smallest one is worse," she said between sobs. Night fell and the men ate supper earlier than usual. Soon she went to care for the child.

By one o'clock in the morning she still hadn't slept, and the child was dying in her arms. Some of her fellow villagers stayed with her that night despite their exhaustion.

"Bring the candle here."

The candle lit up the child's pale face. There was no sigh, no farewell, no moan. Sorrow shut the throats of the family and of the others present. Their lamentations mingled with the sounds of the night among the dense coffee groves.

The funeral was meager. It was a week day, and everyone was expected to go to work. There was no time even to bury their dead. That day Mekel didn't go to work, although it would be one day's less pay. When he returned to the house from burying the boy in the finca graveyard, the three other children were worse, unaware of the disappearance of their little brother. They hadn't realized he was gone, since they were no longer aware of anything.

"You better go back home. The children are getting sicker every day," advised Mekel. "I'm sorry about what has happened to you, it is something that happens to many of us. We are unable to rescue our children from the hands of death, whose main ally is our ignorance and poverty. Only those of us who live with this pain understand and feel compassion for others. We walk the same path, bearing our sorrows, and so we will continue forever throughout the ages."

"Thank you," replied the parents of the sick children. "*Thank you* are only empty words, that we use to express mutual support. We can't fully express the depths of our feelings. There are no words to cover the extent of our sorrow upon seeing our little children go, our little treasures. We've lost all feeling for work, material possessions, and physical pain. Our love for our children was the only thread that kept us alive. Now that they are going, we are left in the depths of despair. Why should we go on living?" asked the mother, weeping.

"We don't know what to do," said the children's father. "We've spent all our money on medicine. We don't even have enough for the return trip. But our relatives in Jolomk'u are even worse off than we are."

"Don't worry," said Mekel, who was echoed by other men who had come back from work. "Tonight we'll have a meeting with some people we know to see how we can help you. It's imperative that you return with the three other sick children. Better to bury them in our village than to leave them in these places."

That night they invited the men from neighboring barracks to talk over the family's situation. They passed a hat around and collected money from all of the people present, who responded generously to their great need. In three days the father would get two weeks' wages and return with their three younger children, leaving the oldest, two boys and a girl. But what to do with the three gravely ill children? They needed help.

Mekel had received news from Lotaxh that the corn in Jolomk'u was ready to be harvested and that it would be a good harvest. To help out the family with the sick children, he decided to make his journey sooner.

On the day they were to leave they gathered up all of their belongings, which filled less than two sacks with old, not very valuable things, and walked to the bus stop. Mekel hadn't had time to buy what he had planned to take back: a little outfit for Lwin, a shawl for Lotaxh, fancy bananas, plantains.

They had to save those three little lives while there was still time.

He tied the straw mat on his pack frame, took one of the three little ones, and returned as empty of hope as he had arrived a few months before.

On the way he helped out as much as he could: sometimes he carried the children, other times he found them something to eat or bought medicine. But the abrupt change from the hot climate to the cold of the highlands made the little ones worse. The journey lasted two days. The first night they found shelter at an inn where they spent the night on straw mats on the damp dirt floor of a long corridor. They wrapped the sick children in torn blankets, but they shook with cold all night long. Long before dawn they resumed their journey in an old bus packed with a great many people piled one on top of the other. With Mekel's help they found a small place in the mass of people surrounding them.

They were laboring up the mountain when dawn broke on the horizon. Most of the passengers were asleep, swaying from side to side.

Suddenly the mother stifled a cry, biting the edge of the blanket. "My daughter has died," she managed to say in a whisper.

The two men quickly calmed her down, before the driver or any other passenger could notice. Carrying a dead person could cause serious problems. They would surely be left on the road or they would be returned to the city to bury the child there.

They had to pretend the child was sleeping and the mother had to restrain her tears. Even mourning aloud the death of her child was forbidden to that mother.

They wrapped the body in some blankets, placed it on the mother's back and continued their journey. There were still two, a boy and a girl, whose breathing was labored like boiling corn. No one could say anything. The sobs and tears rained timidly as dawn came over the cold road.

It was about four in the afternoon when the bus stopped at the muddy crossroads of Jolomk'u under a steady drizzle. The sad travelers got down the sacks and the chests with their personal belongings. Then they got out the sick children. The woman got out with the dead child tied to her back. And the sorrow touching the depths of their hearts got out with them. The bus continued on its way until they lost sight of it down the tortuous road. It went slowly, like someone leaving, never to return. It was a bus of lowest category, rickety, intended to serve the Maya, who formed the lowest of social categories, the lowest of the low. It was a vehicle that could break down at any turn of the road, that could plunge full of people into a ravine and produce both a tremendous clatter in the hills and tremendous silence and indifference from the owners, the authorities and the media.

The roosters instinctively crowed good-bye at the day's end. There was no sun and a persistent drizzle fell. They still had one league to walk on foot and because night was approaching, they had to hurry.

The dead walked deep in thought: some were dead of body, others dead of soul. There was no difference. It was the same, wandering on earth as living dead who receive compassion from no one.

It was already night when the gloomy caravan arrived at Jolomk'u. They informed the village of the tragedy and the news traveled quickly among the huts, from which men and women spilled out to improvise a cold wake for the little girl.

"What happened?" asked the neighbors.

"There were four," repeated the woman, "two boys and two girls. Now there are only two," she said among tears.

That cold wake was warmed by the presence of familiar people, who lent human warmth.

The first burial was heavily attended, as was the second, and two weeks later the third. Sad faces that left without even saying good-bye, leaving a world that did not want them.

The last burial was attended by a preacher who carried a Bible under his arm. After speaking of a God who is good, powerful and just, he concluded by reading a passage from the sacred book: "Truly I say to you, as you did it to one of the least of these my brethren, you did it to me."

A week after the burial of the last child, the couple returned to the finca where they had left the three older children. They returned to the source of all their misfortune, like the fly to honey, without knowing that their feet and wings could be trapped there forever. After selling the little they had, their little piece of land and the family hut that wouldn't last another rainy season, they carried their two bags of belongings and took flight like birds that would never return to Jolomk'u.

A few days later Mekel went with his wife to inspect his corn plants. She had given him a detailed account of everything that had happened in his absence. With his peasant's hands he stroked the spear-like green leaves, that made arches between the furrows, and spoke as though thinking aloud: "Here I'm the owner of my fields, I'm known by my friends and greeted on the roads by the rest. There, I was just one more number with only one thing to offer: my labor. A man's value is as an object or an animal, with the difference that the animal is not demeaned."

"With the help of our God, the Great Spirit, you won't have to go back there," she replied, "because we'll struggle to work our plot here, we'll make our land produce, so that our boy doesn't have to go through such experiences."

Lwin, who was just learning to walk, was once amusing himself in the field, when his soft hands touched a prickly caterpillar that made him cry. The two ran to where the child's cries were coming from. They found him with one hand held up, the caterpillar fleeing up to the top of the corn stalk, inching away hurriedly. After rubbing their son's little hand with saliva they carried him back home.

As time went by, the child acquired new types of behavior. When he got up out of bed in the morning, he would hurry to greet his father and mother. He bowed with his arms folded on his chest and asked their blessing for the new day: "Bless me father, bless me mother," he said. The adults put their right hand on his head and answered: "So be it, son." He gave this same greeting when some adult visited his house or if he met one on the road when he went somewhere with his parents. His bare feet had gotten used to the road full of dust, rocks and sometimes thorns, which poked into his inexperienced feet. Crying, he would ask someone to take them out. His toys were the things that surrounded him: earth, rocks, the corn cobs from which he built little houses, roads and people to whom he gave life.

As he grew, he started learning adult work. In town Mekel bought him a little hoe, a machete for his size, a hat, a bag, and a gourd for carrying corn gruel. He took them to work in the fields, doing chores on a small scale. Many times when he was tired he looked for shade under some bush and fell fast asleep until his father went to awaken him, to eat or to go back home. He ran errands to neighbor's homes and more that once returned crying from fear of the dogs. Later he learned that if he called them by name, they wouldn't chase him, but would wag their tails. For this reason he tried to learn the names of the neighborhood dogs and before calling their owners, he would call the dogs, and they could come out to meet him wagging their tails. When he had to run an errand in the rain, he put a plastic sheet over his shoulders so as not to get wet and he rolled up his pants and put on his hat.

He spent most of his childhood with his dog named "Spot". It went with him everywhere, until the animal died when his owner was eight years old. Many years later he would remember him as one of his best friends, who had rescued him from many dangers.

When he was very small, perhaps five, he told his father, who was coming back in the morning with a load of firewood, that he had had a beautiful dream, and that he wished it would come true.

"What was your dream, Lwin?" asked his father, wiping off his sweat.

"I was with some other children," he said. "There were lots of boys and girls. Everyone had toys, all kinds of toys. They were like real things, only little. There were some balls like the boy who lives at the scribe's house has. Others had toy houses, others sheep, some dogs, and little horses and I saw some that had little cars like the ones people go to the finca in. The children played, ran and laughed. The only one who didn't have toys was me and they didn't let me play. But Spot was there with me."

"Your animal spirit must have been in some Ladino town where there are lots of toys," his mother interjected.

"When are you going to take me to town, so at least I can see the toys?" he asked.

"I promise to carve you some toys when I come back from work this afternoon," said Mekel to comfort him. After that, every afternoon when his father returned, Lwin had him sit down to work on stones or pieces of wood, or put together old rags to make balls. Wanting to speed up the making of his toys, Lwin decided to make them himself one day. He took his machete and started to fashion a piece of wood, and almost cut off his finger. His mother immediately got lime water from the cooked corn and spider webs to stop the flow of blood, and then wrapped them with strips of cloth.

Lwin grew up in direct contact with nature: breezes coming from the mountain caressed his face. The crystalline water of the brooks wet his feet and his hands. He drank that clear water. He grew under the golden rays of sun that began and ended his long days in Jolomk'u. He was delighted seeing the colors of the flowers and of the animals. His ears recorded the songs of the birds, and interpreted their calls in his solitude. He was constantly in touch with the earth.

One morning before Mekel left to go pick corn, he put his son on a mule between bundles of string nets. When they got to Stich'en they met the workers beginning to arrive. There were twenty-five men and women to do the harvest. All the work was done cooperatively. People were notified which day to work and everyone came with hands ready to help, either for construction or farm work. This day was Mekel's turn to harvest his corn and they began. He and his wife had worked hard to get ready. Since the day before she had been cooking corn and preparing lunch for the workers. Mekel had prepared the wood, the nets, and the animals that would carry the loads of corn.

Stich'en was the lower part of Jolomk'u. It was a pleasant place, and perhaps because of that the workers had smiles on their faces and sent their happiness out into the wind with country sounds.

The land where Mekel had his plants was the resting place for the rivers that came down precipitously from the mountains and surrounded Stich'en. It was a place surrounded by small green hills; the green of willows, the green of the meadow where flocks of sheep grazed; the green of the pines and apple trees, as well as the yellow-green of the cornfields like patches on the mountain. It was a pleasant sight. On one side between the cliffs the *mimana'* came down in torrents and on the south another small river came down, which stopped and silently surrounded that cornfield; then the separate streams joined to continue their journey through the mountains.

"This bridge, which is covered with green moss and practically petrified," explained an old man, "was put up by my great-great-grandparents when tall oaks still grew here. The logs are of oak, which is why they have lasted so long." The bridge lay on four stocky logs, which the river licked with its spray as it passed by. The kingfishers whizzed underneath in furtive pursuit of prey. That bridge was a monument to the men who had laid the first stones in Jolomk'u.

The work began. They lined up to go down the furrows of corn, leaving a mess of stalks and dry leaves on the ground. Lwin, who couldn't walk too well between the furrows, ran from one end to the other, answering the calls of the workers. He created a lot of mischief, which made everyone laugh. He looked in each basket and picked out the ears of corn that were shaped funny or had unusual colors and gathered them in a place under the shade of a shrub. Spot ran after him wherever he went.

The roosters marked the midday by looking askew at the sun, which fell vertically on their crowing. Mekel finished the third trip with the eight mules with double nets full of corn. Lotaxh went after him, her cheeks red like ripe apples from so much tortilla making near the fire. She carried a pot of hot gruel on her back and a pot in each hand. A big basket with hot tortillas and two large gourds with more gruel were tied onto one of the animals. She was proud and pleased with the harvest, the product of her effort, and she didn't want to spoil her joy by arriving late with the food. Because of this, she ran after her husband, who was driving the mules. He figured he could make three more trips with the animals, which were beginning to tire from the day's work.

When Lotaxh got to the place, she settled under the shade of the big oak that marked the edge of Mekel's land. She asked her husband to leave the bag with her little boy's lunch. She asked about him, and in order to tease her the workers said they hadn't seen him. But when she called Spot, he barked nearby. The boy was fast asleep under the shade of a shrub among a heap of corn of every color.

The people spread out under the shade, and took off their hats. A light wind refreshed their foreheads under the tree.

The first thing they asked for were the gourds, that were passed from hand to hand to quench their thirst. They served black beans in the clay pots. The round damp tortillas were set out in piles in different spots among the people. In one bowl there was a green chile sauce with diced onion and fresh coriander.

"Please help yourselves," said Mekel.

Among the workers there was a young couple: she was fifteen, he seventeen. She had come with her mother. For these young people this first encounter was like a door opening up that allowed them to contemplate the beauty of their feelings and dreams, caught up in a whirlwind of all those emotions that mortals feel at that time of life. They couldn't communicate directly, with words and sounds, but there was a more eloquent language to express what we call love, which showed itself in various ways.

Since early morning he had been looking for an opportunity to get near her, but circumstances hadn't allowed it, since they were at opposite ends of the line. They only saw one another closely each time everyone got together to empty the baskets full of corn into the nets. They glanced furtively, meaningfully at one another. The two felt the life force in their veins. She was dark with skin polished like a shiny apple. Hair as dark as night fell down her back to below her waist. Her bust lifted up like a wild lily full of the morning dew. Her face was tanned by the high sun. She wore a simple *güipil*, worn especially for work, product of her able weaver's hands. Her skirt reached her ankles, and manifested the ancestral design patterns, which summarized the Mayan world view. On a violet background the memory of the metaphysical world was perpetuated in people's minds, the upper reaches of their conception of the world and of life. The bare feet left their mark on the dust, giving evidence of their delicacy. The movements of her body were in harmony with the swaying rhythm of the corn, moved by the afternoon wind. The boy was a youth with an agile, strong body, entering the fullness of youth, a stage in which the heaviest work was no trouble at all.

But in Jolomk'u, they lived on illusions. Nothing was real, nothing was concrete. Life was a chain of pretenses. For them there not even a modicum of happiness, unless it came out in drops. These were simply dreams, illusions, intense and happy moments to encourage them in their daily struggles. When those who had gone through these stages saw the young people, they cracked a slight smile, and shook their heads as a sign of their own failure. Their advice was to enjoy these illusory moments, a brief pause in the midst of the turbulent life of the Maya.

When they came to work that morning, he approached the girl's mother, greeting her with a nod, and took the opportunity to cast a loving glance at the girl. Her response was to bite her shawl, move quickly, walk hastily, sigh, and whistle almost imperceptibly. They weren't fated to be together in the furrows. There were many people between them, but he did everything he could to show her that he was the best worker. From time to time he got far enough ahead in his work so that he could go to the mother or the daughter's row to help pick. When it was time to carry the full baskets, he would go and get one of their baskets to show his attentiveness.

The sun was rising up above their heads much the same way the temperature of love was rising in their hearts. It was a jumble of feelings, sensations and internal energy that made them see the mountains, the landscape, the work and the people that surrounded them in a new way. It was natural, pure, simple love stripped of the sophisticated masks of the conventions of more complex peoples.

After lunch under the shelter of the shady oak tree, they took advantage of some momentary confusion, and managed to exchange a few words as they passed each other on their way to begin the second half of the day's work.

The lineup of the workers had been reorganized, and they found themselves together. She was in the middle, with him on one side and her mother on the other. They couldn't talk about anything besides work and daily life.

She participated very little in the conversation, but got a great deal of help in the work. There was a melancholy undertone in his whistle, as he lifted heavy nets to load up the animals, and let his aim be known, by flashing signals with his mirror. These were his strategies for impressing the girl.

The workers foresaw an engagement in the not very distant future. They realized the youths' intentions, so much so that the mother of that daughter of Jolomk'u had thought far, far ahead. Her husband had died a few months before, and she had to work tenaciously to survive with her five small children, helped only by that fifteen year old daughter.

Mekel's son was called Little Lwin, because there was a big Lwin and before him another Lwin and a whole series of Lwins going way back through time. As the day ended, the little one had collected corn of all kinds and colors: round, huge, long, fat, thin, yellow, white. He kept them all. One of the ears that he carried in his small hands was one a girl had given him that had the shape of a red heart.

The sun was at a distance of about three furrows above the mountains when Lwin the elder, the grandfather, announced the end of the work and the beginning of the harvest ceremony. They set up a large candle under the oak tree among the nets full of corn. With incense sending out abundant smoke, the old man gave thanks to Our Father God. There was cooked bottle-gourd squash for everyone, and they all got a bag full of corn, taking happiness to the children, who were waiting for them with the fire sputtering as it roasted the corn in the smoky houses.

That day the hooves of the animals had deepened the road that went to Mekel's house. The courtyard of his house smiled amid yellow grain. The attic was ready for storing the nets full of corn. The wooden crosses on the small altar began to be adorned with Lwin's whimsical corn.

"This year Our Father God has blessed us with a good harvest, not like last year," Lotaxh commented as night fell.

"My body hurts from all the work, and I've got blisters on my hands."

"I feel for you. I'm worn out, too. Loading and unloading hundred and fifty pound sacks on the animals eight times in one day isn't easy."

Lwin was growing amidst the strength of the family union and the community. He was welcome in everyone's house and he knew everyone by name. They would all greet him on the road, saying: "Take care, brother." Younger ones like Lwin greeted the elders, asking for a blessing while bowing their heads. Lwin received affection from everyone. His language ability was growing as well as his knowledge and attitudes. His ability in social matters was improving every day: he learned when it was appropriate to speak, that he shouldn't interrupt adult conversation, that on the roads he should greet grown-ups, and that he shouldn't take things that didn't belong to him.

In Lotaxh's free time he would sit next to her and she would tell him: "Respect is the most important thing among people. In order to have rights, son, we first have to fulfill our duties and obligations toward others. We must never trample on the rights of others. Service to others is very important, as our ancestors have taught us. The measure of a person, his level of importance and greatness in our communities depends on the level of service he gives his brothers. Everyone is equal, we're all children of the same father, Our Father God."

"And the scary Ladino, is he our brother too, Mom?"

"When God made the world, the mountains, the sun, the moon and the stars, he made people and he made them out of the same material. Everyone the same, no one superior to another. But with time, some formed groups, divisions and categories among people. Some made themselves superior to others and some were Ladinos and some of us were called Maya. Ever since then the strong have governed the weak, taking away their rights. But before Our Father God all people are equal."

"Mother, tell me how the world and everything in it began."

"I'll tell you some other day, because I need to go feed the pigs, who are squealing in their pen, and your dad will be coming home from work soon and I should fix his tortillas."

Lwin learned that Our Father God existed, but he wanted to know him and perceive him with his own senses.

"Father, where does God live? I'd like to meet him in person. Our Father God isn't grandfather Lwin, is he?"

"Tomorrow I'll take you to your grandfather so he can talk to you about God and show him to you," answered Mekel. Lwin would be instructed by his grandfather about the existence of the Great Spirit.

The next day Lwin insisted on being taken to his grandfather's, which Lotaxh did that afternoon.

Old Lwin said they needed to leave the child three days at his home in order to be instructed about something as important as the existence of the Great Spirit.

That same night the instruction began: the grandmother and grandfather censed their grandchild to purify and sharpen his senses so he could receive the presence of God. They recited prayers and other means of preparation before the wooden crosses in the house. The grandparents began to narrate the history of the creation of the world, of the earliest ancestors, of the arrival of the white man and of the plundering of which the old inhabitants were victims.

"I want to see Our Father God," insisted Lwin.

"Yes son, Our Father God is manifested in various ways, even in the things that surround us. It's the Spirit that lives in every place and in every moment. His presence floods everything that exists, fills the earth day and night, the heights and the depths, the right and the left, behind and before. For this reason, our crosses represent the totality of the universe, the four corners sustained by the presence of God. You can't see God with the eyes of your body, but only with the eyes of your spirit, with your *nawal* that is identified with him and comes from him. When you get up and see Father Sun come from the east, that's where God is. When you walk and see the high mountains, the rivers, the ways of animals, the cliffs, the people we meet on the trail, the birds that fly like arrows through the sky, the fire that heats our food, the air that gives life to whatever exists, there God is manifested. He is in all of his creatures, in every time and in every place."

"When we lift up our hands to the sky and our gaze pierces the depths of the firmament, we are penetrating his dimensions like the birds that navigate through the air. He is our Father. From him we have come, and to him we will return when our days on earth are over."

"The copal, the incense, the candles and the smoke that rise up to the heights are your means of communication with God. They are the presents that people offer out of their poverty."

The last day, Lwin travelled with his grandfather to a distant place, where he had an experience that he would never forget for the rest of his life. He felt the presence of the Spirit, watched and lived with the ants, the butterflies, the worms, the birds, the beasts, the plants. He heard the language of the river, the sun, the wind, the fire, and walked long distances to get to the summit of a great mountain, from where he watched the coming of night with his grandfather.

"See the order with which the Great Spirit has fashioned the universe," he said. "Feel his presence; he has made everything perfect. Look at the infinite world, which is covered by the darkness of night. Hear the voice of God and his language, which is harmony and perfection. Listen to the language of nature, look at the mountains which show the passage of the centuries. Listen now and inside you will hear an inner voice and feel his profound presence. We can contemplate the magnificence of his creation only if inside of us we maintain that same harmony, if we are free of the chains and the burdens which bind our consciences. You should try to be like the birds, like the crystal-clear water, like the innocent worm, like the pure air, like creation, whose perfect order you can behold, free of the weight which drags people down and which doesn't let them participate in this great harmony."

Finally Lwin and his grandfather lifted up their message in the form of smoke and mixed it with air, lifting it to the stars. Lwin was inundated with a sense of sublime grandeur, and he lost track of the time watching the sky, the movement of the earth and listening to his inner voice. He was truly happy.

It was already late when they came back, and the grandfather looked carefully at the road. Lwin felt that he was walking on clouds, and didn't feel the earth beneath his feet.

During the years of his childhood Lwin was educated by his parents in the heart of the community. After the experience with his grandparents, he understood that everything that exists forms part of a universal order, and so he respected all creatures, convinced that they had a right to exist.

He learned that lying was bad. At night gathered around the fire his parents taught Lwin what he should or should not do. The fire was the center of attraction. It gave light and heat and unified those who dwelled within. A hut without a hearth was a dead hut, and therefor they didn't ever let the fire die out at night. Before going to bed, the women banked the coals to keep them alive. They knew very well that fire was sacred, that it came from Xib'alb'a and gave them messages.

Whenever the fire began to sizzle among the logs, the mother immediately realized that they would have a visitor that day or that news of some event would arrive. The fire could foretell pleasant events as well as unpleasant ones, depending upon the interpretations that were given. One morning when they were eating breakfast, the fire gave off negative signals. Mekel watched it with a surprised face. Lwin asked if what was going to happen was good or bad. "Probably something disagreeable will happen today to somebody in the family or to some neighbor," he said. "We have to be very careful," he advised before going to the *milpa*. That day at mid-morning, some men in green uniforms and green hats came to disturb the village and spread fear among the inhabitants.

Lwin, hiding under his bed, thought about the fire that had sizzled that morning. He was afraid of the Ladinos, and those men were Ladinos. They went from house to house, checking in all the corners to see if there were any signs of production of illegal liquor. Everyone knew that those men weren't just looking for illicit distilleries. It was just a pretext to extort and abuse the people. There were deep wounds that never healed as a result of the rural police's visits, which constituted another institutionalized outrage. In more distant places women were raped, husbands beaten, possessions taken without the consent of their owners, false accusations made and bribes exacted.

That day Lwin told his mother that he would use the hearth as an accomplice to make the unpleasant visitors stay only a short while in their house.

"I'm going to get some corn cobs so the fire will really smoke, and they won't go up into the attic and destroy our grain," he said, and did it right away.

"Tie up Spot," his mother advised, "because they use dogs that bark for target practice."

After a long while four of them came, talking in Spanish. Mother and son did not understand that language. All they managed to grasp was the word *kuxa*, which means 'illegal brandy'. They shook their heads, standing in the shade of the entry way.

The men pushed Lwin's mother aside and were determined to come in and inspect every corner of the house. Using a stick with an iron point, they pierced the big pot used to hold water and in a moment the house was flooded. The men took turns coming in and going out with eyes watering from the smoke. This made them even angrier, and they jabbed the lance left and right into everything they saw: corn, beans and lime rained out of the broken sacks. Lotaxh cried at seeing things destroyed that she had managed to acquire with the sweat of her brow. Lwin trembled with his dog at his side, engraving these scenes in his memory. The diabolical laughter of the men resounded from the throats of these representatives of national security and authority.

Once the search was over, which, according to the dead letter of the law, could be carried out only with a proper court order, the men took a bottle out of their knapsack and drank from it.

They continued on their way to another house, and then another. In each one new experiences were being stored in the memories of the children. Those first experiences resulted in a sad and diffident look, interpreted by the Ladinos as suspicion, timidity and unsociability.

Many years later Lwin would comment: "You can't live an adult life with a clear, smiling face, friendly attitudes and trusting behavior when your first lessons of social life came from violent assaults."

That day two neighbors who had bottles of *kuxa* found in their houses had their hands tied and they were taken to town for the respective negotiations. The people cried, knowing for certain that it was a setup, but no one dared to protest.

The hearth formed part of the Maya's life, even on these disagreeable occasions. It warmed their bellies and the tops of their heads from birth. It was a place of rest during free moments, and even at death, it warmed the cold coffin.

Once when some institutional representatives came to convince the community to build raised stoves or stoves of clay, they couldn't understand the opposition of the community. According to the experts, those stoves had many more advantages for the people than their hearths on the ground.

In the first session called by the assistant mayor, the people came to hear the explanation in two languages. The people responded, "Yes. Thank you. Very well." But deep down inside it wasn't easy to pull up the roots of something so profoundly buried in the community's customs and forming part of its very existence.

Up until the time he was seven years old, Lwin had been kept from contact with Ladino culture. On occasion he had heard of more than one sad experience which his parents or neighbors had gone through in relation to this as yet unknown mysterious person. He had the opportunity to see some Ladinos in his village, but resisted thinking about them and tried to let them pass through his imagination like blank tapes. Their appearance was comparable only to the bad *nawal* that comes out at night and takes the souls of dying children: *nawales* that frighten mortals, living in darkness and drinking human blood.

In his sleepless nights he would awaken startled and sweating, talking about the Ladino. He knew that Ladinos lived in the town beyond the limits of his mountains, so he had never expressed any interest in going to town with his parents. His radius of action was Jolomk'u and places nearby. He had a certain aversion to the town, preferring not to imagine that place. It was a fear acquired from his earliest years, when he listened to his parents and to other children's parents say, "If you don't behave, the Ladino will come and get you."

Among his first contacts were with the rural police, the pig buyer, the institutional experts and some Ladinos who had come to survey some expropriated land. All of the contacts left disagreeable memories.

As Lwin grew up he began figuring out in his little head the differences between the two groups. The Ladinos were physically different than the people of his community. Their way of seeing things was different. Their habits and customs weren't the same. The origin of his grandparents couldn't have been the same. Lwin and his people didn't understand the Ladino's language. One day when some people came to buy pigs, it was necessary to go and call the *ajt'zib'* to serve as an interpreter in the transaction, because Lwin's father wasn't there that time and Lotaxh didn't understand Spanish. He realized that Ladinos did not dress like his people did, with *güipiles*, wraparound skirts, necklaces and *capixayes*. Their houses and their food were also different. They heard that they drank milk, ate meat, bread, and the eggs that the villagers took to the market, the best fruit and vegetables, and that when they got sick they used special medicine.

But the big difference that the little one found between his people and the Ladinos lay in their thoughts and ideas. The Ladinos considered themselves more intelligent and superior. They knew a lot of things the Maya did not know, and they could do certain things better. Therefor they were the ones giving the orders and making the decisions. He had heard about a mayor and a Catholic priest in the adults' conversations, and there was even a president that had a lot of power over people.

"Dad," he asked one day, "that face painted on the paper that the men came to paste on all the walls, who is it?"

"It's the face of the man who is going to be president," answered Mekel.

"What does the president do?"

"We don't know what they do, Lwin. There are a lot of things we don't know. The only thing we ask God is that they let us live in our mountains and in our valleys in peace, as the birds and the animals live."

Lwin had discovered that the town Ladinos expressed this imputation of inferiority and devaluation of his people by means of one deprecatory word: *Indians*. He had heard it on occasion, especially when Mekel told of his experiences on the fincas, where there were a great many of his people working. Many times he heard the conversations of his parents when he played in the dirt next to them.

Many times he wanted to ask for an explanation of this

term. It hovered over his head like a question mark. But the adults always tried to avoid it by saying: "When you're grown up, you'll understand." Doubtlessly a theoretical explanation wouldn't be as eloquent as the same practical experiences that scarred the life of a human being.

"The word *Indian*, my son, can't be explained and there's nothing we can compare it to. Rather, it's a feeling that grows inside of you to a greater or lesser degree, according to your own experiences. It's a thorn that most people try to avoid, preferring not to be infected by it. Those that internalize it by mixing with Ladinos, prefer to exorcize it, or set it aside and struggle to free themselves from that identification. When the notion of inferiority that the word suggests grows into a monster, the desperation to flee it becomes even greater, and that's why I say there's no explanation."

"When you grow up, you'll have a chance to see that many of our people make great efforts to try to pull off that black bird clawing at their bodies and their minds. But the harder they try, the more the voice of their indoctrinated consciousness eats away at them, saying: "You're an Indian, you're not worth anything, you're nothing." In the midst of desperation they look for the support of their own people, but they say: "You don't belong to us anymore, you're Ladino, go with them." So they become wanderers, nomads in their own lonely world. They enclose themselves like armadillos in their shells, but they aren't to blame."

"A Ladina woman I know in town told me," interjected Lotaxh, "that when the world was created, there was a long dark night. The Ladinos' ancestors and our ancestors were once together in the same place. While they were waiting for the light of the first dawn, the Great Spirit said that they should find something with which to amuse themselves so they would stay awake and be able to witness the miracle of light. They could ask for whatever entertainment they wanted."

"The Ladina woman told me that their ancestors consulted

among themselves, and our ancestors consulted among themselves to decide what they would ask for in the way of entertainment while they awaited the dawn."

"When they had finished their consultation, the Ladino representative spoke first saying, 'O Great Spirit, we Ladinos have decided to ask you for books, games, art and music for our entertainment.'"

"Then our representative spoke: 'So that we won't fall asleep and miss the light, we ask you for fleas, lice, toothaches, earaches and hard work.'"

"This woman harped on how our people were dumb right from the start and that this is our inheritance."

At his tender age these things worried Lwin. That word was a seed that germinated and sent roots down into the boy's consciousness. Once when he was about eight years old, during the season for burning over the fields, with the air laden with smoke, he was lying on his back in the courtyard next to his mother, who was making a clay pot. He was absorbed in noticing how the clouds were going in one direction and the moon in the opposite one up in the sky, when suddenly he heard his father calling him.

Lwin, bring your stool and sit here, I need to talk to you," he said.

Because of Mekel's serious words, the boy realized that it was about something important. He ran to bring a three-legged stool made from a root. He settled down near his parents, as his mother kept working on her clay. From her look the boy could see that she already knew the reason for the meeting. One of his little brothers crawled close to them.

"Son," began the father, "we wanted to tell you that the assistant mayor of the village came to visit us recently and he thinks that you're the right age to go to the town school. A number of children from our community will be going to school and the parents of those that really can't go will have to go talk to the mayor and pay some money so their child won't have to go. Your mother and I decided that you ought to go for a few years, even if it's only to learn to sign your name, so that in the future you won't be stamping your thumb print on papers the way I do." This news hit Lwin like a bucket of cold water. He had never imagined that some day he would have to go to town to some school along with those children he feared so much.

"There are things you need to learn, son," said his mother. "You need to understand what's written on the papers that you'll be signing later on. Otherwise, the same old thing will happen to you that happened to your father and to lots of people. Before going to the finca your father asked for a loan from a man in town and signed a paper with his thumb print. He left our land title as security, but when he came back with the money the man said that we had sold our land to him, and that he'd let us stay on it only until after the harvest. That's one of many examples of what happens to us because we don't understand what the papers say."

"What did I do wrong? I've tried to obey you in everything like my grandfather told me. Why are you punishing me like this?" protested Lwin awash in tears. "In all these years I haven't gone to town more than once or twice, because I don't want to go where the Ladinos live. No! I don't want to go to school. No! No! No!" he said clutching a house post.

"You won't go by yourself," said his father. "Other children from the community will go."

"Who?" he asked, wiping his tears with his hand.

"Matin Tikxhun and Xhunik Lamon," said his father. "The assistant mayor told us that girls didn't have to go to school, so none of the parents are going to send their daughters."

"My friend Xhapin Xhuxhep is ten, he could go," suggested Lwin.

"That boy's father already talked to the mayor. Last week they went to town, taking the boy dressed in old clothes. They put him in an oversized *capixay* and a torn hat. His face was dirty and his hair uncombed. They pretended he was a deaf-mute. When the mayor and the school principal saw him, they were alarmed and asked questions through an interpreter. But he pretended he didn't hear; he just shook his head. They were convinced and took him off the list."

"Xhapin isn't deaf or dumb," said Lwin.

"No, but they need him to work at home, so they made this arrangement with the assistant mayor, who was given two hundred pounds of corn in exchange for serving as a witness."

"Hey, that's a good idea. Let's do the same thing," proposed Lwin. His parents said no.

Lwin spent the next few days sighing, alone, sad, not playing and with no appetite.

Lwin would have to walk about four miles between Jolomk'u and the town twice a day. The mountain of Watx'ona' rose between the two places, so that it took an hour and a half to travel those rocky roads.

Mekel and Lotaxh sacrificed their own needs and the needs of Lwin's sister and two brothers to buy his school supplies: a string shoulder bag, crude leather sandals, a straw hat, a wool *capixay* and two pants made of cheap material.

The day came to go and register. That January 15th would be remembered by Lwin for the rest of his life as a day of the most intense contradictory emotions. He didn't sleep all night. There were circles under his eyes, and he felt no joy in wearing the new clothes they had bought him. He followed his father as if walking in his sleep, with tortillas and a bottle of cold coffee inside his bag and his heart full of fear.

Any traveler in an emotionally stable state would have perceived the town as very beautiful. The town was encrusted on the face of the mountain range. Wachwena' was the port of entry to the numerous villages spread among the distant hills. The town was in the lap of the valley that started at the foot of rocky mountains, wrapped in a cloak of smoke that peacefully spread over the settlement. The white church stood out, as well as the town hall and some of the larger homes. The valley extended even farther, to be lost in the purple distance. On the slope of one of the mountains surrounding the town, was a white cemetery like a patch on the green. A gentle river flowed between the houses, on its way to where the sun comes up. All the tiny roads converged at the same point: the town.

They rested for a while, looking at it, and Mekel took advantage of the pause to scrape the strap of the new shoe, that was making blisters on his son's feet. Neither one spoke.

"Tonight we'll put some lard on it," said Mekel.

They fell silent again.

That January 15th was a Friday. There were no regular classes yet, since they were still registering, and the teachers who lived far away had gone back to their homes.

So many children! Lwin had never seen so many children together. They ran from one side to the other, running everywhere. Most were Ladinos.

There was a building with wooden plank walls and on the opposite side another building with a big passageway. It must be the mayor's office, which he had heard of several times. They went to the building, took off their hats and went into a room with wooden plank floors. In one corner a Ladina woman sat behind an unpainted rustic wooden desk.

After Lwin's father exchanged a few words with the woman, she took out a book. Then he heard something that must be his name, because at home they had said his name in Spanish was "Pedro Miguel."

That had been the moment, he recalled later, of beginning to have a double personality, double attitudes, a double name, a double way of acting: one way with his people and another with the Ladinos.

That day they gave him the choice of staying overnight at the school or returning to his village. He preferred to go back with his father. On the way back his father told him what he had discussed with the teacher, saying that he had been registered in the Spanish-as-a-second-language class.

Lwin was used to getting up long before dawn. By sunrise he was usually already coming back from fetching firewood from the forest along with his father. When classes began he continued fulfilling this responsibility.

The first day of classes he ate his tortillas after bringing in the wood. His mother gave him more tortillas with beans in them and a half a bottle of coffee for lunch and he left for town. He went up the mountain quickly and came running down the other side. He walked like a deer through the streets, avoiding the Ladino children, arriving at school by a round-about way through solitary places. He was sweating, most of the other children had arrived, and the teacher was dusting off the rustic table. There wasn't any room left for him on the few benches. The ones who arrived last remained standing, leaning on the walls, or squatting on the wooden floor.

The first thing Lwin did was to go to where the teacher was, take off his hat and bow his head to greet her as they did in the village. Most of the students burst out laughing at the greeting, especially the Ladino children. Visibly upset, the teacher lifted up Lwin's head, and began to say things in a disagreeable voice. Her gestures and expression gave the impression that she was angry, practically yelling in the boy's face.

Among the words he succeeded in hearing was the one he had tried to put out of his mind: *Indians*, as well as *customs*, *foolishness*, *good morning*. Those last words she said very insistently, shaking the boy with her hands on his weak shoulders. Eventually he figured out that he should repeat that and finally said: "Good morning."

When that cruel welcoming speech was over, she told him to go sit down. With his face turned toward the floor he went back to the darkest and most distant corner of the classroom.

As he reacted with chills, his shirt which was stuck to his skin dried with his body heat. Remembering his mother's instructions, he tried to pay attention, but that day, just as on many that followed, he couldn't understand anything. During recess he went to stand at the end of a long open hallway, trying to get a little sun. Standing apart from the others, he recognized two children from his village who had been attending school for a week and he came timidly up to them. He was able to find out about life at school and what behavior was expected, although his friends were in the same shape he was in. He learned to greet people saying, "good morning," and learned the official name of the teacher to whom one should say *señorita*."

There was a conflict within him. He didn't know whether what he had learned at home and in his community was right or the new things he was learning in school. It was a conflict that required him to make decisions and choose one or another alternative way of behaving.

Many times he wanted to give it all up and go back to his people, but his parents wouldn't allow him to do so.

After recess, the teacher took roll, and when she called "Pedro Miguel" no one answered. One of his friends told him to say, "Here!" He did so, remembering that in school this was his new name. This evoked another comment from the teacher and laughter from the students.

The teacher was a woman of about thirty-five years of age. She had three children, one of whom was five years old. Most of her time was devoted to her own children. The smallest one busied himself making life miserable for the other students. With his mother's approval, he would take their things away and play with them, but the teacher was very intolerant of other students. She had taught in a number of towns, and was from the departmental capital. She traveled there frequently, neglecting the students. Usually she was gone the first day of classes, and the last day of each week. Lwin was able to avoid having to walk to town on those days, staying home to help his parents.

The abrupt change from his family environment to the Ladino school environment was very painful for the boy, because they were two totally different worlds. Years later, some friends who had left school agreed that they dropped out, not because their family needed their work, nor because they had to migrate (considered a principal cause in official circles), but the real cause of the high dropout rate was the incompatibility between the ways of seeing, feeling and doing things. It was the anguish of degradation that they felt in the midst of something that wasn't theirs. Consequently, depending on the intensity of the influences, they suffered different degrees of lowered self-esteem.

"I always felt anxious with teachers, who were strangers among us" one of them said, "when I had to speak, think or act, because I didn't know if I was doing the right thing or not. This strangled my freedom until I was finally convinced that these people were superior to me and that I couldn't aspire to be like them."

"For me," said Lwin, "the school and the family were two worlds, two life styles and two self-concepts. On weekends I would begin to get used to the happiness of being home, but then I'd have to give it up on Monday and go to school with a false personality and artificial customs."

"I couldn't take it any more," put in another of those talking and reminiscing. "After two years I chose to return to the security of my family, because every day I saw the values I had acquired at home in childhood being shattered. So I turned around and sought out my own people."

"Not me," said another of those speaking. "I put up with it. I wanted to become like those of the other culture, and as a result I felt alone and abandoned. I tried to run away from myself, but the more desperately I ran, the more something inside myself chased me. I compared myself to those cats whose tails we bad kids would tie a tin can on. The more they ran through the streets the more noise the can would make."

The few village children required to attend school in town were quiet, inattentive and shy, and they did not communicate with the others. At recess they formed their own separate groups, sharing their disadvantaged position in the community. They did not talk much, nor did they play, for in the village play was not a part of their normal activities. Back home, no one played. From their earliest years their play was working with little tools. They were content to sit out in the sun and isolate themselves from the ridicule of the town children, who threw things at them, snatched their hats, shoved them and teased them. On more than one occasion the sleeves of Lwin's *capixay* were torn off.

One morning he needed to leave the classroom. His need was urgent, but because he did not know how to ask the teacher's permission, he decided to sneak out before he had an accident, as had happened to some of his friends. After a few minutes he came back very worried, trying not to be seen. But just then the teacher went to the door with her wooden ruler, which she routinely carried to "dust off the *capixayes*." That ruler was the teacher's trusted assistant for bringing order into her school. They had affectionately dubbed it the "pinch-hitter," and the children hated it with a vengeance. Few of them had escaped its caresses on different parts of their bodies: heads, hands, shoulders, or legs. The ruler was crude, darkened with age. It had been with the teacher for a long time in the different places she had taught.

The teacher had the strange custom of rewarding students' good behavior by allowing them to take the "pinch-hitter" home over night, and then to have the privilege of using it on their fellow students the next day. Perhaps she did this to assuage her own conscience or because she was tired of this method of correction.

For the teacher there were four levels of misbehavior according to severity, each with a corresponding type of punishment. One was simply the use of the ruler on the fingertips or palm of the hand. Another punishment consisted of making the children kneel on gravel or corn for a long time. Another was to make them stand under the burning rays of the sun or in the rain with their hands up until they couldn't take it any more. There were children in poor physical condition due to poor nutrition, who fainted under these crude educational techniques. What did it matter? Most of them were Indians.

That morning when Lwin returned to the classroom, the teacher was upset.

"And *vos*, where did you go? Who gave you permission to go out?" she asked.

"*Vos*," answered the trembling boy.

"What did you say, you dumb Indian?" replied the indignant teacher. "No Indian is going to call me *vos*, because we're no way equal, we're not the same at all. You are insolent, abusive, rude, disrespectful." Each adjective was accompanied by a whack on a different part of his body.

The boy understood very little of what was said to him. As his punishment, he spent the next three mornings sweeping the long hallway.

The only word that Lwin had known up until then by which to address another person in Spanish was *vos*. This is what he and his companions called each other. And now it turned out not to be the right form. He was really disconcerted and didn't know which language to use. The teacher herself used that expression when she spoke to them. But they couldn't address the teacher that way. Lwin had used the expression out of ignorance. Having no other alternative in his limited vocabulary, he used the only thing that he knew.

With the passage of time he came to understand the significance of the expression that had made such a mark on his life. He finally discovered that there was a *vos* that went two ways and another that went only one way. One established a common understanding between two equals as an expression of confidence and equality. But there was another one that marked the great differences of status, culture, economy, race and power that was exercised by a social superior over an inferior. Submission and unconditional acceptance was required on the part of the inferior. It formed part of Lwin's teacher's mental scheme and was what he heard in town, at the market, in the media, in the courts and in many other places.

A long time later when Lwin's people had a better understanding of their own values, and had a positive evaluation of themselves, the following story was told.

There was a Mayan woman selling her vegetables in the square and a Ladina asked her, "How much are your potatoes, María?"

"Twenty centavos a pound, Marcela," answered the seller.

The customer immediately protested:

"My name isn't Marcela."

"My name isn't María, either, lady," replied the other.

The years went by coming and going every day to the town school. Each day there were new experiences and new frustrations on the long road of adaptation to Ladino culture:

language, ideas, ways of thinking and acting. He had to transform them into his own world and translate them into his own thoughts. In his desire to adapt one form of life to the other, anxious indecision arose in the boy, who saw school as a means of advancement as well as a barrier interposed between himself and his people.

One of the two companions from the village who had started school with Lwin dropped out the second year, because he could see no use for this kind of education. Besides, there was the long distance he had to go to school, four miles, twice a day. The other student carried on with his fellow sufferer. They went up and down the lonely trails hundreds of times. They knew each turn by heart, each shortcut and each path. In the afternoon except during the rainy season, they would go fetch firewood after returning from school, so as not to have to get up early the next day. Sometimes it was firewood, other times it was fodder for the animals. They fulfilled their duties at home, but they didn't always have the resources to do their homework.

"I think that I'm becoming convinced we Maya are dumb," Lwin's friend commented as they were coming down the mountain one afternoon.

"Why do you say that?"

"If you look at our grades, you'll see that all these years we haven't been the best students."

"Do you think this is because we aren't very smart?" asked Lwin.

"It's possible. We've heard it so much, I think I'm even beginning to believe it," answered the other.

"I don't think so," replied Lwin. "In fact, I think our poor performance in school is due to a lot of other things. We help our parents with their work. We don't have all we need in order to study like the other children our age. For example, we don't have a house like theirs, with plenty of light, and a table and chair for doing homework. We don't have school supplies or enough time, because we have so far to go. Nor do we have adequate food, just cold tortillas and cold coffee for lunch. If you look at it, we start out at point zero. Plus we don't understand the language, or know the way of thinking in which we are being taught. Our health is poor because we aren't adequately fed and we're outdoors in bad weather. Our parents can't guide us and help us because they themselves didn't go to school. We lack the basic necessities at home, and under these conditions we can't be expected to do well."

One afternoon when Lwin got home, he was more exhausted than usual. He still had his tortillas, having lost his appetite. He just nibbled at his food and went to bed to sleep. His mother was worried and said so to Mekel.

"He's not eating; he brought back what I put in his bag," she said.

After being scolded for not eating, Lwin decided to give his tortillas to the dogs he met on the road in order to avoid unpleasantness in the future. He wasn't hungry and each day his health was getting worse and worse.

There were some gradual changes in those boys. They didn't greet the elders of the community. They lost respect for Mother Corn, throwing tortillas to the animals. They started to use bad language. They looked for excuses not to help with the work at home. Sometimes they would play hookey and wander around in the forests, killing birds with slingshots. Their homework, in general, was poorly done because there was no one to ask about it and because they wrote at night by faint candlelight with their notebooks on their knees.

The first few years he tried to study until late at night, beside his mother who was mending clothes. That didn't last long because very soon his eyes started bothering him, until he got to the point of not being able to read for more than a few minutes at a time.

Lotaxh, worried about his eyesight, tried to cure him with drops of lemon or orange rind in his eyes, and passed a cat's tail over his eyelids to return them to normal. The *curanderos* prescribed a remedy he took for several weeks and it helped cure him.

The first three years he learned to read and write, but he understood very little of what he read. One day Mekel had a very important paper to sign, and needed know what it was about, so he called his son.

"Read me what the paper says," asked the father.

"All right, father." Lwin began to read fairly well, but when he was done reading the document he noticed the faces of a number of people there: no one had understood the document. They had to go to town to consult other people. The vocabulary in which the document was written was not within the scope of Lwin's limited Spanish.

As the years passed, he became accustomed to the system of education. A human being can adapt to all kinds of circumstances, no matter how difficult, he commented later.

"We're like Mother Corn," he said once when he was an adult. "We adapt to all climates, to all times and all altitudes. We've created our own defenses against suffering. The wounds heal, but they leave many scars on our spirits. They are internal and invisible wounds which we carry for the rest of our lives."

Lwin was fifteen when the teacher called Mekel to talk to him about his son.

"Boy", she began, "your son is already in the sixth grade. He's one of the few who will finish school. Of the eighty that started in first grade, only five will finish this year. That's the norm, otherwise, what would we do with so many educated Indians? There wouldn't be enough people to do the work."

"I called you," she went on, "to tell you that this year you will have to buy uniforms for the Independence Day celebrations: pants, a shirt and jacket. As always, the school will take care of having the uniforms made and we'll tell you how much they cost as soon as possible."

"Thank you, ma'am," answered Mekel. "Could you please tell me how my son is doing in school?"

"Look, you Indians don't need much. You don't need a lot of education to cultivate the earth, plant the cornfields, carry firewood and weave your *capixayes*," she answered. "Besides you're real dumb, and you don't remember anything you're taught. That's why you drop out. A lot come and try for a year or two and then they leave. They weren't born for intellectual work but for the carrying strap. It's not worth it, it's like wasting gunpowder shooting grackle birds," opined the teacher. "And, oh yes, we're asking all the parents to pitch in and donate what they can: corn, beans, eggs. Those that can't will sell lottery tickets so we can raise funds for the school."

"Yes ma'am, we'll help. Thank you very much," said Mekel as he left.

The help the teacher asked for was sent the next day. Lack of cooperation was one of the things very much taken into account at school. There were some students that spent each year without any trouble thanks to their practice of this ethic encouraged by the school, that is, making donations.

Matin Tikxhun, the friend who had started school the same time as Lwin, was also finishing up his last year in school. They had shared both happy and difficult moments during those long eight years of elementary school. Each one was making different plans for the future. A scholarship had been offered to Matin by some foreign missionaries to continue his education in the departmental capital. Lwin, on the other hand saw the struggle his family was going through trying to keep the family afloat and decided to help them with their work. One of his goals was to transmit the little knowledge that he had gained at school to his brothers and sisters so that they wouldn't have to go through the same unpleasant experiences. He taught them words, the names of things in the Ladinos' language. He made an effort to find the necessary time to teach them basic literacy skills.

During the last months of the school year, the rains were unbearable. It rained night and day, at all hours and everywhere. The hills were being washed away, brooks multiplied and formed wrinkles on the face of the earth. Large quantities of fertile soil were dragged down by the great rivers.

The schoolboys' clothing was damp on their bodies. Their *capixayes*, still wet from the previous day, were put on again to go out in the hurricane-strength winds.

One afternoon the two friends were coming down the hill they traversed twice daily under the buckets of water that had been falling for three days. Lwin's hat was old, for Mekel no longer had the money to buy him a new one. Water ran down his face like little creeks over mountain slopes. The water was dripping through the holes in his *capixay* and running down his back. His sandal straps were torn from getting wet and coming loose so often from the mud that swallowed his feet up to his ankles.

Everywhere there were rivulets of red clay. The bag with the notebooks under his arms was soaked. The wind played with the plastic sheets on their backs, which no longer protected them. They walked without caring about that, talking about their future plans.

"Matin," Lwin said to his friend, "you'll keep on going to school and I hope that when you've reached your goal of becoming someone, you won't change your attitudes and behavior, and forget about the people you're leaving behind. If you can do anything at all for us, don't be ashamed of us nor deny us; that will be enough. Never, my friend, become an oppressor and scourge of your own people. I'll never forgive you if you do. Don't be like someone I met a while back who was walking next to his humble mother, but when he saw some friends of his, left her, pretending not to be related to her."

"I heard about a boy," chimed in Matin, "who went to

boarding school. With great effort his parents managed to save up enough money to go visit him. They arrived at the prestigious school and asked for their son. The boy visited with them in an out of the way place for a very short time, explaining that he couldn't spend much time with them because of the pressures of school work. The parents went back home very disappointed, regretting not having been able to spend more time with their beloved son."

"His schoolmates asked if they were his parents. 'No', he said emphatically, 'they are some peons from the finca that my father sent to bring me some things.'"

Neither one said anything for a while. The wind continued playing with the plastic sheets sticking to their backs from the storm.

"I'm not going to go on in school," began Lwin. "I'll stay here in the village. If you can, sent me whatever things you think might be useful to me. I intend to keep studying with books. Otherwise I'll forget what little I've learned."

"I promise. I'm sorry you can't go on, but I know that our financial needs are greater than our desire to get ahead."

Lwin's personality at that age was being shaped like a jigsaw puzzle printed in many colors. His experiences and personal history formed the basic underpinnings of his adolescence, as he was growing in between two different worlds and two counterpoised foci. He tried to decipher the attitudes and behavior of the Ladino. He made an effort to analyze his own life. Flashes of hope cut through his solitary sky, as he dreamed of the symbiosis of the two cultures working together, building good relationships and a real nationalism to reach up to the azure sky like the ancestral temples, built on solid rock.

At the end of eight years of school he stopped to analyze and evaluate the alien education he had received in town and the simple, humble, but authentic and real education he had received in his community. He didn't have ambitious goals.

He would stay in his community to support his people shoulder to shoulder and try to use the positive aspects of his education for the benefit of Jolomk'u.

In spite of his firm desire to cling to his own, those eight years had exercised a significant influence on the youngster, who had prematurely become a man. At his age he had already seen a wide spectrum of the sufferings of the world and had accumulated a pile of defeats, without knowing the smiling face of life.

Once, on All Souls' Day, two young people, a brother and a sister, came to Mekel's house. They had come to Jolomk'u to put flowers on their dead relatives' tombs. They looked for their relatives, but they had left the village months before to find work on the fincas. Since they found no one, the two asked to stay at Mekel's house. No one recognized them, for they had left so young. Now they were alone, homeless, without parents. They had come to their village to bid farewell and fly away for good.

They were the only survivors of the family which had returned to bury their three children in Jolomk'u, one of whom had died on the road. The parents had returned to the finca and had been buried there.

After losing their parents the pair had moved to the capital. He sold little things on the street; she worked as a domestic.

As they unraveled the story of that family, Lotaxh dusted off her memories. She could see the scene fifteen years earlier when she was saying good-bye to Mekel. Out of the mists of time the truck began to roll, and a girl with her bundle on her shoulder was struggling with her dog, who didn't want to walk. Coming from out of the mists of the past, that same girl was now standing before her.

The two young people had changed in some very profound ways. They didn't speak the language of Jolomk'u', Q'anjob'al, so they could communicate only with Lwin and Mekel. Lotaxh could only watch them, because she didn't understand Spanish. The clothing they used, their manners and even their names had changed. They had adopted the traits of city people. The people of Jolomk'u looked at them as strangers and asked who those two young people were.

"This girl didn't speak a single word of Spanish when she left and now she doesn't speak our language. How can you forget something you're born with?" asked Lotaxh. "Where is her language, her dress, her customs, and her values which give support to a person in society, give life and nourish happiness?" they wondered.

"Do you think they're happy?" she asked.

"I suppose not, mother," put in Lwin. "but basically, they aren't at fault for what happened to them. There are hundreds of thousands like them walking around. They are the product of the idea that they put in our heads from childhood, that simply because we're 'Indians,' we have no worth. A time comes in our lives when that conviction takes hold of us, and we do everything in our power to abandon everything that identifies us with our roots. We turn our backs on our own people and hold out empty hands begging for foreign traits, trying to rid ourselves of our own. This doesn't produce happiness, only more depression and a burden of remorse. We admire something outside of ourselves. We are dazzled by the foreign: if a person is Maya, he aspires to be Ladino; if he is Ladino he longs to be foreign. We never worry about building up our own selves. It's not true that these people can't speak their own language, nor do they have a better life than ours. Many of them live in worse conditions than those of us here in the village. What has happened is that they have been mesmerized by the lure of the city, and they stay there doing whatever they have to in order to survive. Most of the women work as maids, doing the more difficult housework without fair pay or benefits, without receiving adequate and respectful treatment. They are the objects of disdain, insult and humiliation. They are seen as objects and not as people in most cases. The men don't develop any special skills, but eke out a living selling any old thing, wandering the streets with their families. They can't aspire to a higher-paid job, since they have no training for it. They live in slums without utilities, swelling the ranks of the unemployed."

"Mother, all these feelings of inferiority begin right when a person is born. School, religion, politics, are all components of the system that silently suppresses our culture. They are like drops of rain that become small rivulets when they fall on the earth. The rivulets join to form rivers with larger and larger channels."

"When you come into the system, the first thing you have to do is put your values aside. It's like taking off your clothes and putting on someone else's."

"If it's a question of religion, they take away communion with your God from your mind and mouth with one blow. This God is the one you can find always and everywhere, whom you consider your friend, the only one who understands your misfortunes and your fears, who you can dialogue with, wherever you are: in the forests, on the mountains, on the cliffs, in the farthest and nearest places of your life. Then someone comes and tells you that you have an idolatrous, polytheistic, pagan culture. They burn your crosses, destroy your incense burners, tear down your places of worship, make you bend your knees and your head to make you recognize as legitimate a strange God with the color of your oppressors' skin, with your oppressors' language. This God doesn't understand your language, and to communicate with him, you have to memorize something alien to your feelings and intentions. Finally, like an injured dog coming to his master, you take refuge in what they have imposed on you, carrying a book under your arm that you don't understand and that is interpreted according to their whim. Your senses, which were fruitful in prayer and communication with the Creator, with the Great Spirit, become blind, deaf and dumb. This fruitfulness and eloquence withers and dies without voice in a world of silence.

"If it's in education, they mock your collective dignity. They characterize your leaders and your ancestors as an ignorant people, with a rudimentary technology for farming, hunting, fishing, and transport. They rarely speak of a civilization and a culture that established some of the fundamentals of universal science and technology. They emphasize the negative aspects of history and the social sciences. So you feel defeated, useless and convinced you're nothing. They teach you from the time you're small that only a dummy like Tekum Umam would get it into his head that rider and horse were one. There you are portrayed as defeated, gored by the brilliant sword of don Pedro de Alvarado, the white leader with a title of respect. There you are, thrown down, looking up at your executioner, with a white face, blue eyes, blond hair, coming in the name of "his" God, whom you should worship in the churches and carry on your shoulders in the Holy Week processions so that you'll feel inferior always and everywhere, and accept whatever the cross and the sword impose on you."

"And your values and your nationalism? It's the task of the educational system of every country proud of its citizens and of its history to promote them. Where are those that speak of our nationalism and our country?"

"Why don't they gather the scattered fragments and begin to mould a new society with brown and white hands, where color, form and size are relegated to second place? As long as they don't unravel the entangled skeins of the races and accept the fruits of the past without being ashamed of themselves, there won't be any development."

"When we turn our faces back toward our own values, we will sing hymns of triumph and glory. We will labor to build on the foundation of our own identity, our own patterns, our own style of progress and development. Then there will be brotherhood, and we'll forget resentment and hate. We will all raise up Tekum, who is still stretched out with his green dreams, flitting above his body sleeping in the silence of the centuries. Coming from many places, we will unite our hands to break the chain of dependence that ties down our quetzal bird, which still has the color of hope and aspires to fly freely. As long as we don't sit down to drink a cup of *chilate* for peace and brotherhood, as long as some laugh at and mock others from their respective positions, as long as some use others only as objects for their own benefit, the separation will turn into an insurmountable abysm."

"I think you're dreaming. I don't understand," put in Lotaxh who yawned, listening to her son's monologue.

"I'm sorry, mother, maybe I am dreaming. A lot of people won't understand me or will prefer to turn deaf ears to my words. What I'm trying to say is that as long as we Maya passively accept everything that they impose on us, without full, conscious, and reflective participation, a lot of years will go by before we can understand these things."

"What things are you talking about?"

"Mother, it's hard to define them because they don't fully belong to us. In school I learned a song whose meaning I don't understand, a song about the flag, that represents beautiful ideas, but just ideas. Some patriotic symbols represent what a person should be, but to up to a point they are just symbols; they never become real. Some holidays: Independence Day, Mother's Day, Columbus Day, Arbor Day, and I wonder: What independence? Whose mother? For as a peasant woman, you are only the mother of pain, tears and work for all of your life. Ever since Columbus came, we have been an abandoned and rejected race. Everything they taught me made me think, and I ask myself: who made up these things and with what purpose in mind?"

"We plant and care for trees so that others can come with their trucks to take our wood. But woe to us if they find us cutting down a tree for firewood.

"Do you believe, mother," he continued with tears in his eyes, "Do you believe that this education has made me great and liberated? No way. The further I go in these studies, the greater is my disappointment. It would have been better not to have gotten their education at all. At least that way I wouldn't have become conscious of my reality."

A strident noise interrupted the conversation. The two guests were returning to the house after having gone to swim in the river. They had long hair and dark glasses. The young man had tattoos on various parts of his body and the woman wore minimal clothing. They arrived moving rhythmically to the beat of rock music, sounds disagreeable to the quiet community of Jolomk'u.

● ● ●
___

The *municipio* was one of the largest in the region. It covered an expanse of mountains with its more than thirty villages, where more than fifty thousand orphaned children of the Maya lived. Because of their distance from the urban centers, public services were deficient, or rather did not exist at all. There was a great deal lacking in the villages, and much poverty. There were minimal services in agriculture, health, education, housing and work. The official agencies were not very productive, on account of their heavy operating expenditures, that is, to pay for the bureaucracy, which not only lacked the necessary resources to do their work, but also for the most part lacked any interest in doing it conscientiously.

Programs and projects were like castles in the air, without a sound philosophical base, or definite and adequate policies adapted to the reality of those populations and their real aspirations. The officially approved plans and programs were imported from places and societies with a world vision different from that of Jolomk'u.

No one wanted to go work in such a distant area and those that did, hoped to get transferred to a city.

The alleged experts that sometimes came were really just apprentices that had come to experiment, or people sent to a distant place as punishment for their mistakes or inefficiency. No one stayed very long, for the discomforts of the place quickly made them go stir crazy.

The employees were left to their fate by their bosses without guidance or adequate planning. They spent days shut up in their offices filling out stacks of forms to justify their stay: sending plans, reports, requests for equipment and supplies that never arrived.

They often spread the bad habits of their own social group, setting poor examples for the local populace or perpetrating scams. They showed little responsibility in their work. On the other hand, the people of the community didn't pay much attention to them. They preferred to use their own traditional agricultural and health care practices instead of wasting time in boring meetings.

The people said: "Mere words can't help us eat, we need concrete action."

One Sunday, taking advantage of the fact that a crowd of people had arrived from all of the villages, the local officials went through the crowd ordering them to gather in front of the town hall at 10:00 a.m. to listen to the mayor's regular speech.

The people, mostly men, gathered at the appointed time. Up on the platform was Mr. Diéguez, who had a monopoly on local power, because of his servile relationship with the current government. Taking the microphone, he addressed the public.

"Boys, I called you together to greet you in the name of the legitimate Constitutional President of the Republic, elected by you." The "legitimate" president mentioned by the mayor was the strangest earthly product, shaming the human race. This executioner was without peer. By his orders, the most horrible methods of torture and death had been used. Hundreds of thousands of Maya cried out for justice against him.

"In response to my request," continued the mayor, "our government, which is concerned about the needs of its people, has sent us a team of agricultural experts to improve our crops.

They will visit all of the villages with town officials. When they arrive at your community you will need to take care of them appropriately. They are going to teach you how to use the new fertilizers for sale here in the town hall," he said. "I will now turn it over to the project coordinator," he concluded.

"Gentlemen of this beautiful town," he began in unhurried fashion, "My name is Alonzo. I am a specialist in plant science, with a degree from Harvard University. I have carried out research for over five years in different countries. At present, I am the coordinator of a project to improve the varieties of corn in the western highlands. This geographic zone is included in a long-range program of research that will shape the entire system of macro-economic development in this country."

"As you know," he continued, "a project of this magnitude requires that we proceed methodically, beginning with research into local needs, a diagnostic process in which each and every one of you will play an extremely important part, a *conditio sine qua non* for the success of the project. It's a tripartite project, financed by three international organizations. The experts I will be leaving with you will help those communities which can be reached by road. You will need to feed them when they arrive at your villages," concluded this expert, in order to allow time for translation into the local language.

The mayor began to yawn.

A murmur spread through the crowd, wondering who this stranger was. Some said that he was a governor, others that he was a candidate for president. Those who were farther away asked what language he was speaking. When the speech was over, a burst of applause rose from the assembled peasants. Then they listened in silence as the interpreter consulted with the mayor as to what message to give.

"These gentlemen have come from far away to help us improve our corn and beans," he said. "We must provide food for them when they arrive in our communities; we have to prepare meat. But don't worry, because they'll go only where cars can, and you know there aren't many villages with good roads. The mayor says that what we really need to do is buy the fertilizers here at the town hall," the interpreter concluded abruptly.

The sale of chemical fertilizer was one of the mayor's own personal businesses, and he was taking advantage of the presence of the experts.

The farmers from a few villages attended the first meetings with great enthusiasm, leaving their agricultural work on various occasions to go to the workshops. But the experts didn't show up or got there late, leaving all responsibility to the local agent, whose only function was to serve as interpreter.

When the experts came to the meetings, they brought films, slides, posters and other media created in an urban environment with an urban mentality. Often they were materials brought from other countries by people ignorant of the local community, which simply didn't understand them or their messages.

They were promised new and better seeds, but the seeds arrived after planting time, which was late that year, thanks to the unfulfilled promises. The seeds that came did not germinate because they were too old. The demonstration plots that were set up as models for applying the new agricultural techniques were placed in strategic places, and so the techniques didn't yield the expected results. The harvests of the farmers using traditional practices were more plentiful.

And so the farmers became disillusioned. They quit attending the meetings and did not believe in anything that had been promised. All that remained were large loans for fertilizers they had received, and in time many of the farmers lost their small parcels of land, as their title deeds had been left as security for the loans.

Finally, the experts left the villages or were chased out by the people. At the last meeting in Jolomk'u, to which only the agent came, the farmers declared: "They've only come to deceive us and promise us a lot of things that they didn't follow through on. They came to create new needs among us and to cause us problems with their seeds, fertilizers, and new techniques, that you don't even understand. They're nothing more than theories taken out of books, and they've never really worked here. Tell your bosses that it's their fault we've lost our harvests, our foord and even our lands."

The scribe began to talk: "We need new knowledge to improve our production. But more than anything else, we need responsible people and not charlatans that come to see what they can take away from us and plunge us deeper into misery."

The scribe, indignant, continued: "How many years have official experts been coming here, living comfortably and spending public funds on vehicles, gas, salaries, travel expenses? And what have they accomplished? What have they contributed to the progress of the towns? What are the results of their work in the different areas to which they have come? We can't lift our voices in protest because there is corruption at every level and woe to him who dares denounce these things, for the dignified functionaries will be offended."

"When one wants to do things well, everything is possible," commented one of the people attending the meeting. "My grandfather told us a story when we were small about when he was forcibly sent to do construction work on the south coast. He said that there was a president who was very strict. He himself went out to see if people were obeying the law. Once he ordered the chief of police to disguise himself as a peasant and board one of the loaded buses at a certain place, to check to see if his subordinates were doing their job. When they stopped at the police checkpoint, the driver's assistant prepared the papers for the bus. Before getting out, he asked the driver how much of a bribe he should give. 'Are there three policemen?' asked the driver. 'Yes, there are three' 'Give them two apiece,' ordered the driver. Six bills were placed between the papers. The police who had made them stop didn't bother to inspect how many people there were, staying a good ways away from the bus."

"The moment they took the money, the chief, who was in disguise, ordered the security guards, who were mixed in with the passengers, to arrest them. In a few minutes a van came for them and the three policemen were relieved of duty."

The people hearing the story were cheered.

"I don't think you need some kind of superhuman initiative to control corruption," commented someone in the group.

"I think the people bear part of the blame for allowing these things to happen," said the agent, offering his opinion. "We should denounce every incident of abuse."

"My friend, we could spend our whole lives denouncing every kind of abuse, and they still would never hear our voices," replied the speaker. "First, they would call us enemies of the nation instead of considering our complaints and suggestions. They would say we're resentful, maladjusted, frustrated, etc. They use a lot of sophisticated terminology for these types of behavior and attitudes."

"This is the work they are responsible for, those who plan, those who supervise and give guidance, those who control. That's what they are paid for. How is it possible to leave in the hands of the public something that is their responsibility? It's clear that no one can demand something that they aren't capable of practicing themselves. Corruption is a disease that they criticize when they are ordinary people, but when they get power it's the first thing they catch."

They spent hours talking about various cases in the community: the food, which instead of being distributed to needy people was sold to businessmen; the school supplies that supposedly were sent for underprivileged students, but went for other purposes; grants to the town government, that enriched only a few; the housing, the land, the loans.

Everything reeked of a sickening corruption.

"Just talking about these things helps to get them off our chests," noted one man with many years of experience in such matters, "but hoping they'll change someday is a real dream. I've seen governments come and go, all with the same old story. When they come and ask for our votes, which is the only thing they're interested in, they offer you the stars."

"It isn't in their interest to change things," said a woman kneeling in a corner. "Do you think that if our lives here changed, there would be any motivation for asking for any more aid from the rich industrialized countries? What justification would there be for traveling all over the world squandering the public's money? Our homes, our suffering and our ignorance are the real reasons for their large incomes. In the world there are people and nations of good will that think we are the beneficiaries of their help. But out here help from the outside is a drop in the bucket."

"There's a typical pattern found in our towns and in our government," said another wanting to get into the discussion. "For example, they go crazy building clinics everywhere without adequate planning. It seems it's the buildings that are important, because after they open them, they leave them in charge of a few employees with their little boxes of aspirin and miracle pills, which they prescribe for all kinds of illnesses. If a woman comes in because she's pregnant, aspirin; if you have a fracture, aspirin. But on the news we hear on the radio, they talk about millions for various great projects."

"We've got millions all right: the lice, fleas, and parasites in our kid's bellies and millions of dead filling up our cemeteries," concluded one woman.

"When there is good will and when you want to do things right, everything is possible," put in the same older man. "Notice how differently some of the private institutions work, like the parochial school or the dispensary a block down from the clinic. Every day they are full of people that leave satisfied with the attention they got and with the medicine that comes directly from other places, while government employees spend the day inactive and bored. But it won't be long before they start preventing this help from coming in, because the rich and powerful complain that their exorbitant incomes aren't high enough for them."

"It's sad when we're just considered objects useful for meeting the needs of government officials," commented another older man. "Not long ago, our elders and our religious brotherhoods were brought together for the purpose of making a trip to the capital. They were sponsored by some institutions holding sway over the villagers. The brotherhoods didn't know why they were going. The most respected man of our community went along, but when they got to the city, they were left at a low-class hotel where there were brotherhoods from other towns with different clothing and different languages."

"Despite his inadequate Spanish, don Paltol, for such was the name of the respected elder, was able to find out that the reason for the trip was the arrival of some people from distant countries to whom they would exhibit the rich culture and folklore of our people. They were probably representatives of those friendly countries that were always sending money."

"They asked our elders to perform some of our Mayan religious rituals, which as you know, are sacred and can't be toyed with in a meaningless fashion. Then they had them march by the National Palace in front of the visitors, who took lots of pictures."

"The foreign guests enjoyed witnessing the vestiges of the great civilization which once flourished in these parts. After the parade, the government offered a banquet in the palace at which toasts were offered to a people that wasn't even there. They sent the elders back again to the hotels with the lousy service and the next day told them to go back home."

As night was falling they adjourned the communal meeting,

in which they had spoken a little bit about everything. Then they returned to their homes under a shower of stars.

In Jolomk'u all major tasks were undertaken collectively. This was no institutionalized cooperativeness in which one group manipulated the majority. This was spontaneous cooperation, disinterested, natural, with a basis in mutual service and brotherhood. The sowing of corn, harvesting, house building and road repairs, were all community activities. They just had to let people know ahead of time, generally on Sunday, so that the neighbors could plan their weekly activities.

It was the season for clearing the fields, and it would soon be time to sow. It was hot, and the land anxiously awaited the first April rains. The men of the countryside were happy when the black clouds lifted and the snail kites flew in long lines through the sky, announcing the coming of water: it was time to sow. The swirling winds played with the dry leaves from the cornfield that went soaring to the heights, and then fell like silk ribbons at a fiesta.

One hot afternoon, Xhapin Anton went out on the dusty road from hut to hut to say that in three days he would need the community's help in planting his corn. He prepared digging sticks for thirty men. They were thirty tools for burying in the bosom of mother earth the handfuls of seed corn. He shelled the best ears of corn reserved for seed. Then he got the elders together to communicate with the spirits who intercede before God on behalf of the plants.

In the midst of the seeds, with the candles lighted, with the censers giving off the aroma of *pom*, the elders lifted up their voices under the dome of nature:

"Come nigh, ye Spirits: B'en, Chinax, Tox, Elab'. Come, bless and protect the sacred seeds. Drive the coatis, the moles, the birds, the armadillos and the other wild animals away from our seeds, so they can grow. Ye lords of rain, lords of air, lords of fertility, protect Mother Corn so that we won't lack for food and can serve the Great Spirit, God with all his powers."

While the elders were praying, the thirty men were sharpening the digging sticks with their machetes.

The squad of thirty men began their work by simultaneously sinking their sticks into mother earth, depositing the source of life, each man invading the prepared earth within the furrow. Handfuls of seed were buried in the hope that they would sprout with all the force of life, pulling up through their roots the essence of the earth.

Lwin was there, reintegrated into the life of his people. He was a man now, sharing a life with them, and the happiness of breathing the air of his Jolomk'u.

But there was something in the boy that made him different. Not very communicative, he preferred being alone more than necessary, quiet and absentminded. His laughter did not have the clarity of the others. It was as though eight years of absence had taken away the authenticity of his spirit, had robbed part of his dynamism. There was an invisible veil over his countenance, a flat tone to his voice, an opacity to his movements.

"Lwin, you're love sick over some Ladina woman," teased the boys his age. The jokes became more frequent. They threw things at him, they laughed at his clumsiness of his work.

"Lwin, you think you're different from us because you can read and write," said one boy.

"No," interrupted another, "he's got a crush on Petlon. I saw him signalling her with his mirror the other day when she went down to get water at the well."

"I don't want to talk; I got a headache," was Lwin's excuse.

"Maybe you're forgetting our language, like those who leave the town and then come back speaking only Spanish," added another.

A roar of laughter spread through the men planting.

"I don't feel like joking now, so please don't bother me," the object of the teasing managed to say.

"Yes, you have to leave him alone so he can figure out how to use the planting stick. Maybe you could plant better with a book," mocked one of the boys.

"You're right," answered Lwin. "I'd like to know if somewhere there might be a book, or someone with a new and better way of planting corn, so we don't have to go on pecking at the earth like this, wasting time. I wish at school they had taught me that instead of the nonsense I stuffed in my head that has been of no practical use to me at all. Eight years lost, and then they give me a piece of paper that doesn't help me earn a living. What good is it for me to know that there are different continents, famous places to visit, beautiful port cities, art and science from other worlds, if I hardly know my own people. I hardly have enough to survive one day after another."

And addressing the one who had spoken before him, he said:

"And you, my friend, I warn you that the next time you say I've turned into a Ladino I'm going to have to remove that idea from your head the way I would dig out an chigger with a needle."

"If you can't manage a digging stick, how do you think you'll be able to change my opinion of you?" answered the other.

Lwin was visibly offended and said, "With these," showing his fists, at the same time attacking his adversary.

The shouts of the men was like a concert of *chocoyo* birds invading the cornfield. Some egged on Lwin and others Xhapin. The sticks were stuck in the ground, all in a row, waiting for their owners.

It was a body-to-body fight. Their arms and legs were entangled, as they rolled down the hill, sweeping aside the dirt and leaving the weeds flattened. They fell down, they got up, they rolled some more. Blood trickled out of a corner of Xhapin's mouth. Lwin's cheeks began to swell from the blows.

Two adult men came running to put an end to the fight, one of them being the owner of the field:

"I don't want a poor harvest on account of the blood shed at the hour of sowing. Step back and forget this unpleasant episode," he said. "We still have a lot of work to do, everyone to their places," he commanded. Several young men had to intervene to separate the two hot-blooded boys.

They continued the work in silence. All that was heard was the noise of the sticks striking the earth as they opened up little mouths to swallow the seed corn.

Lunch time came. They sat down in the shade of the bushes and ate without speaking. Only the work leader interrupted, asking them to serve themselves.

Such was considered normal behavior among boys. The tense atmosphere diminished quickly with some new jokes, taking care not to refer to what had just happened.

At the end of the day, under the sun's last rays, they made the usual bonfire of dried twigs. The men threw handfuls of corn among the embers to make popcorn, eating it with bowls of black corn gruel.

Xhapin took the initiative, approaching Lwin to apologize for the incident. Lwin got up, put his hand on his companion, and the two of them walked up to some rocks, sat down and talked for a long time. They didn't partake of the popcorn, but even at a distance one could tell from their gestures that the conversation must have been interesting. The rest of them said good-bye, and they followed behind over the rocks until the night covered them all.

●●●●

It was nearing Eight Chinax, the sacred day for building houses, with adobe for the walls, wood and straw for the roof, and there would be a housewarming.

Nikol Lapin and his wife headed up a household of many children, six boys and five girls. Four of the sons were married and had children, and everyone lived in the same paternal house. The problem of overcrowding was creating difficulties among family members. They urgently needed to build more houses, especially for those who already had their own families. Nikol's land was being subdivided more and more.

His wife Katal was kneeling next to the smoking pot with the cooked chayotes, which she distributed among the grandchildren surrounding her. The men had returned from the fields after a hot day of work. Old Nikol absentmindedly plucked some hairs from his beard, as his vision ventured into infinity. On his knees he held the smallest of the grandchildren, his namesake, for whom he had a special affection.

"Honey," she began, "don't you think it's time for our children to have their own place and their own cross, so they can live separately with their families? This house isn't big enough for all of us, and the women are starting to squabble over the children."

"You're right. I've thought a lot about it. Some nights I

lay awake thinking about it. When the roosters crow the first or second time, my eyes don't want to close any more, and my imagination goes chasing after the problems. During the dry season we need to build two small houses for our children with families. Within two weeks it'll be Eight Chinax. That day we'll gather the people to make the adobes."

"In the meantime, we should consult the diviner to avoid any danger. Let there not be any accidents, may Mother Earth let us build our houses, and may the mountains give us their trees for the roofs."

"We'll go visit the diviner in three days," decided the old man.

Three days later they were on their way to a neighboring community, where lived the diviner who gave guidance concerning all matters.

"Sir, we want to build huts for our sons, their dwelling places, their refuge on Mother Earth. Speak with the spirits, consult them, throw the *tz'ite* beans and count them to discover our fortune."

After waiting a while the old man rolled up his pants in such a way that the veins of his calves would show.

He waited in suspense.

His eyes were fixed on the veins jumping in various places, one of them convulsing under the old man's skin.

"Ah," he said. "I see. Yes, there's a vulture gliding over the peaks of tall mountains covered with leafy pines. I see also unity personified, that which follows the zero of our ancestors. Unity is the beginning of the road of life and being. Again the vulture, drinking drops of blood falling from the sky, flies through the air in pursuit of the drops.

You should immediately settle accounts among yourselves," advised the diviner. "May your sons and daughters-in-law kneel before their parents and before you in the presence of the crosses, amidst the smoke of the *copal* and of the candles. Ask for forgiveness, admit your faults, and listen to the confessions as you stand holding bunches of wild plants, which you will place on the graves in the cemetery, so that evil will be banished from the new houses."

It was done.

The first task consisted of making the adobes. Then the foundation of the house would be laid almost a lunar month later. Then they would bring wood from the high mountains and finally, all of the neighbors would put the straw on the roof .

When everything was ready, they sent word out to neighbors and friends.

They came on the appointed day to the appointed place, near a rushing river that ran between cliffs. The women came to the house of the owners to offer their help.

Four sheep with twisted horns hung from the beams. They had been slaughtered for the occasion. The women bustled around performing the many necessary tasks. Those who had small children would take breaks to squat down and breast-feed them. The children pressed against their mothers' backs cried from hunger, and from the smoke which pulled tears from their eyes.

"Take your milk, my son, I've got lots to do," they said while they searched their hair for lice eggs. These were little breaks in their work, a change of pace. Once the break was over, they wrapped the children up in cloths again and put them back on their shoulders.

Meanwhile some of the men with pants rolled up above their knees kneaded the mud with their feet. Others brought water in clay pots. There were some who brought the mud on a wooden litter to the molds, and the rest had the task of forming the rectangular adobes by dividing the mud into squares on a large flat space under the sun. The shouts, the laughter, the atmosphere had the festive air of peasants playing with dirt.

At mid-morning a group of women arrived with pots of

corn gruel and netted bags full of gourd cups. The ones carrying the pots were two young girls with bare feet and faces like ripe apples. Those carrying the cups were grown women, one of whom would be the owner of one of the houses being built.

The girls aroused much interest among the young workers, especially Lwin.

He volunteered along with two others to pass out the cups of hot *chilate*. By now the men were tired and thirsty.

The young girls were shy under the young men's gaze. They played nervously with the ends of their braids, biting the shawls they wore. They blushed, staying close to the women.

Lwin's heart had been calm up until then, but it began to wake up. A certain rosy-cheeked face with an innocent and timid mouth, was destined to be the fire that would melt the ice that had petrified the boy's heart and feelings. Destiny and the gods seem to have provoked that encounter.

She realized that Lwin was interested. She also felt somewhat the same. She was young and at sixteen her intuition had developed like a sixth sense, alert to the tormented moments of love.

Later, at lunch time, among the crowing of the roosters, they drank, tilting up cups of corn gruel. The workers ate it along with bowls of red chile.

In Lwin's deepest emotions there was a hidden seed of frustration, that not even he could fully identify.

"Why does my soul grieve?" he wondered.

His anxiety had something to do with the absence of the beautiful, innocent face that had flashed before him that morning like a shooting star. He looked in vain among those bringing lunch, but she wasn't there.

There was one more possibility of seeing her, during the afternoon snack of corn gruel, but she didn't come then either.

"Lwin, count how many adobes we've made," the owner

of the work requested.

He immediately began and counted more than two thousand adobes. They were satisfied with their work.

The sun was four fingers above the mountains.

"Let's rest, men," said the owner. After a little while the men went down to the river to wash themselves and their hoes.

By now they spoke less than at the beginning of the day, the fatigue being shared by all.

The man working as a mason gave instructions on how the construction should go: "Our homes have had the same style since olden times," he said, "It's part of our tradition: it's the way our ancestors did it. A rectangle eight yards long, by six yards wide and four high. The main door should face the west. On one side a window no more that one yard square and, if you want, another smaller door to one side."

They set aside the next day for going up into the mountains to bring the wood for the houses.

Communication with God on the hill, the cemetery, and the mountain was intensified by the efforts of Nikol Lapin and his wife, who went everywhere carrying candles and other supplies for the prayers.

"Lord of the forest, lord of the mountain, you who know everything, keep us from danger, deliver us from the evil intentions of the Ladino. Let us not be deceived and fall into his traps. See, Lord, we are poor and defenseless. Only you can perform miracles so the Ladinos won't notice your humble servants. We ask you for good health for our neighbors and relatives. Care for the workers that bring the wood for our little homes, a refuge for our children. The vultures that wait in ambush for us night and day, may they be banished by your great power." They went to consult the diviner once more, and he kept seeing the same thing.

"Be very careful, the vulture is still there, making circles in the sky over the mountains. When the veins on my left leg announce something, usually something unpleasant happens. I don't want to frighten you, but you should take precautions. Tell the men to be careful."

Chinax was on its second cycle around, twenty days having passed since the adobes were made. They had dried and were stored ready for the building.

Yaxantaq, the virgin forest where conifers grew wild, was three hours away. The men would go there to fetch the beams, the cross beams, and the uprights for the houses that they were about to build.

The strongest men of the community were picked to do the hard work of going to get the big logs.

There was a full moon in the night sky. At the first crowing of the roosters the men left their warm straw mats while the tousled women prepared the coffee and the tortillas for an early breakfast.

With axes and ropes on their shoulders, more that twenty men went out to Yaxantaq. There were whistles, shouts and the barking of dogs. They were silhouettes coming out of the houses in the dim light, like *nawales* walking on the roads. The youngest got ahead of the group, whistling in the night. Two of them were far ahead of the rest talking the talk of youth about their plans and projects. They wanted to prove their strength by being the first to arrive, showing an avalanche of youthful enthusiasm that could be seen in their work every day. From time to time their machetes could be heard against the dry branches and the rocks in the road.

It seemed like daytime, for they could see things a good distance away in the moonlight.

Then they entered the thick forest, the huge branches forming roofs over their heads. They went slowly over the small paths traced through the undergrowth. At that hour the morning frost was falling. The birds warmed their hanging nests attached to the branches. One could hear the intermittent singing of birds. They kept climbing toward the summit, from where they could see the villages sleeping down among the shadows.

They left the dense trees at the top of the mountain, and made their way to a clearing in the forest. In the midst of that deep quiet, far from the nearest villages, with no trace of human existence nearby, two white figures suddenly appeared about three hundred paces in front of the incredulous eyes of those intrepid youths: two maidens dressed in white *güipiles* that moved with the breeze. Their loose hair fell down around their shoulders, their speckled wraparound skirts shone as they walked. The brilliant full necklaces that adorned their necks reflected the moonlight.

"Two women out alone at this time of night?" queried one of them.

"They look like they're coming from a fiesta," replied the other.

"The nearest town is twenty leagues from here. It's not possible."

A chill ran down their spines all the way to their feet. They didn't know whether to go on or to stand petrified where they were. They were convinced that no women from any village should be walking in such a place in the daytime, let alone at this hour of the night, especially young unmarried women. Nevertheless, the girls kept coming toward them, engaged in a lively conversation, judging by their gestures.

"What should we do?" asked one of them.

"Let's approach them slowly. There are probably men right behind them."

The distance between the two couples was getting shorter and shorter all the time. The figures that had seemed fuzzy were now more clear and definite. They were two beautiful women with their hair partly covering their faces.

Two hundred paces away. The young men slowed way down, their bodies heavy, their throats dry, their skin with goose bumps. They wanted to shout and run away, but where to? There was not even a single rock on the great plain behind which they could hide themselves.

A hundred paces away. The figures kept coming toward them. They approached as though on clouds, without walking. Now they seemed to be moving through the air, over the grass.

Now they were only about twenty paces away, face to face on the very same path. When the women passed by a shrub just off the path, the boys heard someone sobbing behind them.

They looked back for a moment, then scanned around for the women, but they had disappeared. They cut down the shrub with their machetes, but found no one.

A terrible chill took hold of them. Then a fetid odor invaded the place, and they could not stop vomiting until they sat down on the grass, shaking in a cold sweat.

Much later dawn began to show behind the distant hills. Small groups of men began to arrive with breath steaming out of their mouths. They walked to where enormous pines grew in a straight line up to the heights, seeking the sky. It was like a wheat field swayed by a morning breeze. The oldest trees creaked as they moved, and dry branches split off from the treetops.

The guide led them to the summit among rocks full of moss, where there were five enormous trees that had been marked several days before by the axes.

Teams of five men got together. They took off their *capixayes* and hung them on the bushes.

Two by two the men began to cut each trunk in unison. An explosion of birds flew out in all directions, and the echoes multiplied.

"Move in two more," said the leader.

The first ones had mended shirts soaking with sweat. Fifteen minutes went by, and the second group chopped thick chips of wood from the trunks.

The fifth man in each group had the job of using his axe to direct which way the tree should fall.

"Wait a minute," said the man directing the operation. "The trees should fall one by one. Hold the rest, just this one for now," he indicated. "Be very careful."

The leader delivered the final blows of the ax: five, four, three, two, one. The enormous tree began to lose its balance, producing a rushing sound that little by little turned into a storm full of heavier and heavier hailstones, until it passed by dizzily, bringing down the branches of other trees with its leafy top and came to lie stretched out lifeless on the mattress of underbrush.

One by one each of the five trees fell.

Once each tree was felled, the men proceeded to cut off the branches, leaving only the trunk. The last tree was almost the cause of a tragedy, as it suddenly changed direction, spinning on its stump and falling onto another tree, and then toward a group of workers.

"Watch out!" they shouted.

Two men were whipped by the tips of the branches.

The rays of the sun were diluted as they fell on the lush green carpet of moss and ferns.

Once the branches were cut off, the men began to pull the logs toward the slope, and then down the hill. They walked on ahead, opening up a path through the underbrush, with some of the men removing obstacles in the way. The trees slid down with ever-increasing speed. The men moved to one side to watch the five trunks speeding by and finally coming to rest at the foot of the mountain at the outskirts of the first village.

There were others that were supposed to help take the trunks to the building site. The enormous logs would be pulled with strong ropes and round logs serving as rollers. Men had been selected to carry the trunks around to the front.

The job would never be completed.

Many months later the five trunks were still lying motionless like mute witnesses to the cruelty of man against man. The forest ranger was there with five deputies, witnessing the arrival of the lumber.

They were armed to the teeth.

"Nobody move," they said. "Who's in charge here?"

"I am, sir. We have a permit," replied Nikol Lapin.

"No one told me anything about it. Where's your papers?"

"Yes, sir. Here they are." He opened his bag and took out some papers wrapped in a red kerchief.

The official scarcely looked at them and then tore them up in front of everyone.

"Tie up the old man and his two sons," he ordered. "The rest of you go home if you don't want to get into trouble with the law," he concluded.

The deputies tied up the three peasants.

"But, sir," spoke up the eldest son, "the mayor gave us a permit for cutting five trees."

"Maybe," answered the forest ranger, "But in this area you didn't just cut five trees, but a lot more than what was authorized. Get going. We'll see how many logs there are up there."

When they counted them, there were more than one hundred and fifty logs which had been cut months before. It was a business in which that very ranger had conspired with lumber dealers in the capital.

The old man kneeled down before the ranger and with his hands clasped together pleaded: "Sir, I swear that up until today we never came to cut even one little tree. Just these five today for which we have a permit."

"No," he said, "You're shameless liars and thieves. You can see for yourself how many trees have been cut and you still dare to deny it."

One of the boys who was tied up came up to the ranger and whispered something in his ear.

"It's too late now," he said. "You should of thought of that sooner, not after I caught you red-handed."

They headed for town.

It was past noon when they came down to the first villages. People shook their heads and were quietly indignant when they saw the three men walking in front of the ranger, mounted on his horse. The deputies held the ends of the ropes in their hands as they all walked toward town.

When they passed through Jolomk'u, a group of men and women near their homes beseeched the officers as a last resort, and offered corn gruel and tortillas to the prisoners.

The official remained steadfast.

"Get going, it's late."

They returned the cups half full, swallowed the last bites of tortilla and continued on their way.

At the town hall the mayor consulted his secretary, who furnished him with the relevant laws.

The prisoners had been charged with the excessive cutting of more than one hundred and fifty trees, causing deforestation and depletion of the flora and fauna of the country, which are offenses against the renewable and nonrenewable natural resources of the nation.

Because of the seriousness of the case, the mayor determined that it could not be resolved at the local level, but needed to be taken to the court in Huehuetenango, the departmental capital, to have a greater impact on the suspects.

The villagers convened an urgent meeting to seek a solution to the problem before the three men were transferred to Huehuetenango.

"In my opinion," said the *ajtz'ib'*, "we have to send some people immediately to the mayor's house, not his office, to talk to him. And if we can, we should talk to the ranger; maybe things can be arranged at this level. Even if they have to sell some of their animals or a piece of land, it's better than a long, drawn out trial in the departmental court."

The same scribe along with three other men from the village went to the mayor's house. They waited more than one hour, because the man was taking his nap.

After listening to them, he pretended to be inflexible and zealous in seeing to it that the laws were enforced. He waited for the opportune moment for the unhappy Maya to sweeten his ears with the customary offer of a bribe.

"Look, fellows," he said in a more compassionate tone. "You're all dummies. When I gave you the permit I told you to talk to him," referring to the ranger. "He's an authority too, so don't screw him, you guys."

"I know it wasn't you that felled those trees," he said, taking his victims' side, "but the report has already been submitted." The mayor pretended to have no interest in what the peasants might offer him.

"I'll talk to him and see what he says. Meanwhile, the rest will stay in the jug."

He was going back to his office when he pretended to remember something and came back a few steps. "You know, it's a bad situation. There are one hundred and fifty logs as evidence up there, and they're not going to hit you for less than twenty per tree, plus legal expenses. Add it up." Saying this, he disappeared.

Later, protected by the darkness of night, the two officials began to drink a little and set a price for the matter that appeared attractive to both.

"They're going to do us a favor and take care of it here," was the first news that came to Jolomk'u.

"How much?" asked the crying women.

"Five hundred, not a penny less."

Days went by.

By the fifth day they managed to scrape together the necessary amount by selling their few remaining sheep, a piece of land and a few hundred pounds of corn and beans intended to feed them for the rest of the season. The remainder was made up by a collection taken up among the neighbors.

They arrived at the mayor's office after it was closed, when all the employees had left. Only the man in charge of the jail was still there awaiting orders.

"Let them go," said the mayor dryly.

It was night when the men came back down to the village.

This incident completely changed Nikol Lapin's plans. The houses would be built with the simpler materials that could be found around the community. The walls would be made of wattle-and-daub construction and the cheapest wood, with a roof of straw. The adobes were still waiting, rows of them forming trenches, which collapsed, forming little mounds on the ground with the passing of time and the effects of the seasonal rains.

The wounds in the collective spirit were shared by each and every one.

So continued their timid life, as they tried to forget the humiliation and abuse, but basically it was not possible.

They wondered whether in other places, in other societies, life was similar to theirs: whether rational human organization depended on the few and the destiny of the many depended on those same few. Were these the results of the system that they had heard the political parties preach and defend so much? Was this the way democracy was in other countries or was it only a self-serving and corrupt interpretation?

They wondered about many other things as events proceeded.

They managed to build the first wattle-and-daub house with a lot of effort and planned to invite the whole community to a housewarming, to the extent their financial situation permitted. The diviner indicated that Chinax was the day they should hold the ceremony for "planting" a new cross for the family.

"Children," said Katal Elnan with a breaking heart, "It's time for you to have your own place. We would like to give you something better, an adobe house, so that the cold winds of dawn wouldn't blow through the cracks, but we can't afford it. It is time for you to go and live with your little children somewhere else. I'm really going to miss you, but it must be done. We've put together the things you're going to need, so you won't lack for anything in your new place: a grinding stone, pots, jars, baskets, benches to sit on. We'll make pole beds for you to sleep on. We also bought you a new machete, a hoe, a carrying strap, an ax, and other work tools.

"Take care of my grandchildren, bring them up the right way, as we did with you. Set good examples for them, for there is no better way to teach than by setting an example yourselves." It was just a few days until the housewarming, and the grandfather, the grandmother, the son and his little family were all together.

"Thank you, mother. Thank you, father," they said. "We thank you so much for what you're doing for us. We don't deserve it. If you like, we can go on serving you in our father's house, but if you've made your decision, so be it. Forgive us our transgressions and those of our little children. Perhaps we haven't always carried out your will faithfully, so please forgive us."

"Whatever is on the land and in the new house belongs to you. We hope you'll be happy with your family, who will serve you someday as you have served us," said the grandfather.

This was said a few days before the housewarming.

The third day at dawn five men went toward the mountain in search of new crosses, including the two grandfathers, the diviner, the scribe and the owner of the new house. Once again men and women came to take part as soon as it was light. There was joy each time there was some group activity. The children formed groups to play with sticks and stones or went dashing out to go on some small errand or complete some task, such as sweeping the house with brooms made of branches.

The women had a chance to talk about various aspects of daily life. Some men went to bring pine needles to decorate the place and others slaughtered animals, taking their entrails to wash in the river. Everyone had a job to do.

As the morning went on, more people arrived to be with the family. Everyone was waiting for the arrival of the cross.

"Put the pots on to boil. They're going to come back hungry," advised the grandmothers over in the corners.

Meanwhile, up on the mountain, they were walking among the trees looking for the tree which would fill the requirements for becoming a cross. The diviner guided the group, concentrating often so he would know in which direction to look. Finally, his veins and his divining instincts told him where there was a short red pine with branches twisted by the years. They came to where the ancient tree grew amid the rocks.

"This is it," said the old man, signalling with his cane. "Take out the candles and the incense burners." The candles and the incense were lit. Five elders prayed under the shade of the trees while the owner of the house took his ax and began to cut down the small pine. They cut two pieces a yard and a half long each, then came down off the mountain in a cloud of tobacco smoke: the owner of the cross in front carrying the two pieces, followed by the elders walking slowly.

It was past noon when they came back to the little house.

The two pieces of bare wood were placed on a rustic table.

The women knelt on their straw mats, murmuring prayers to the two sticks. They had gone to meet the men in the courtyard with the incense burners, who walked backwards into the dwelling and stayed in front of the wood that was to be carved later on.

Under the diviner's direction, the carpenter began to carve the wood, making a symmetrical cross.

"We don't know when, where or exactly how," began the diviner, "this sacred cross originated. It may have been from the beginning of the world, for our forefathers conceived of the universe in this manner, representing the All, known to us as God, the maker and the shaper. The four ends represent the four corners of the earth spinning around the main axis, who takes in everything with his presence.

"To have a new cross in each home is an act of immersion into this spiritual world, submitting to the will of God and gaining his protection."

More people arrived after a large firecracker announced the return of the men from the mountain with the pieces of wood.

The carpenter finished his task; then the most important ceremony took place as evening fell. The new residents came forward and knelt before the old men, who remained standing. The oldest began to recite the history which had been told and transmitted from generation to generation, starting when the world first opened its eyes and humans were created in the image of the Creator. Then he spoke of the places through which the ancestors moved and their sufferings in different worlds until they settled in that place. He told of the arrival of the white man, who stripped their people of all of their possessions and exiled them to distant places. Their descendants were the Ladinos, who continue to abuse and humiliate them.

Then the old man began to analyze the new methods used to break up the community, the new techniques used to take away from them all they had: their culture and traditions.

"What I'm taking about are the systems designed to make us all think alike in such areas as education or religion, whose sects multiply more each day. Then there are political systems that create new needs aimed at converting us into consumers of material and spiritual products. They're trying to integrate us, absorb us into their culture without respecting our freedom and our right to just and equal interaction. But after many centuries they still haven't succeeded. They talk about integration into a system where one is superior to others, but they have never spoken of equals constructing a new society and a new nation."

The old man's jaws were tired from so much chewing on words with an ancient flavor. It was more than two hours of history, analysis and orientation for those in attendance.

Finally the grandfathers and grandmothers placed their hands on the heads of the kneeling couple and made their supplications, which lasted another long stretch of time. As they finished, two people helped to lift them off their knees and sat them on benches.

It was dark outside.

"Come in, please sit down," invited the grandfather.

There was a large table on which they placed the gifts brought by the guests.

Two men, each with a bottle of brandy and a glass in their hands, served drinks, beginning with the elders, who were seated with their heads tied in kerchiefs.

A marimba echoed the crying of those who had so much to cry over in their lives. The notes of the *son*, fashioned from sadness and pain, set the mood for the gathering. The collective tears fell on their hearts, gradually saturating them.

The liquor pushed down the lumps in their throats, until they were changed into dances full of feeling and pain. Everyone savored the nostalgia, moving their feet slowly and rhythmically on the pine needles scattered about the floor.

The feet, the movements and the feelings began a dialogue with the music. It was part of their world, a language that communicated what could not be expressed in words. Everyone danced, adults and children, men and women. They had to take advantage of this moment of distraction in midst of the harsh village life they lived.

After a few more *sones*, they sat down to eat: little yellow-corn tamales, soup with red chile, everything nice and hot. They didn't eat all of the meat: some was saved in the bottom of their bags to take home, even if just a bite for family members that could not come.. They wrapped them in *kanac* leaves, the same wrapping used for the tamales.

"Please help yourselves," repeated the hosts. "Have a little more soup, my friends. Help yourselves, everyone, give the children some more," they suggested.

Everyone was busy at that long-awaited supper. They sat as much as possible in small family groups in a circle. Those who still couldn't eat by themselves received mouthfuls from their mother's hands.

Just then a young man came in, who went to the elder's table and nodded to them one by one in greeting. Then he took a bottle out of his bag and gave it to one of the grandparents. The latter got up to thank the young man and invite him to sit down.

The man, with the pretext of greeting his acquaintances, went everywhere as though he were looking for someone in particular. He had on a new *capixay* decorated with colored thread, new leather sandals and blue pants. He had a red kerchief tied around his neck.

The smile on his face gradually disappeared as he went through the corners without finding the person he was looking for. He was sure he would find her there, but his hope was quickly fading. All of a sudden he was sorry he had come to the party.

"Have a drink, Lwin," said the host.

"No thanks, I don't drink," he answered.

"I know you don't drink, but this is a special occasion. It's the only way I can repay you for all the favors you've done me," insisted the other.

It was truly a very special circumstance for Lwin; he needed the drink.

The liquor went down, scraping Lwin's gullet. Then he wiped his mouth with the back of his hand.

"Thanks," he said. They quickly brought him a bowl of soup and little tamales for his supper.

When the supper was over, the marimba once again played music with the same rhythm of the *son*.

Lwin went near a group of friends to pass the time. He had no intention of dancing. He went up to one of the young men, a close friend and asked: "Have you seen them?"

"No, I don't think they came," answered the friend.

"I've looked for them everywhere and can't find them."

"Have you been to the kitchen?"

"It's the only place I haven't been, but what could they be doing in there? Everyone else is out here dancing."

Just then the sister of the boy Lwin was talking to passed by. They called her over.

"What's happening?" she asked.

"Have you seen our host's younger sister? She was with your friend the day they were making the adobes."

"No," she answered and walked off carrying some bowls in her hands. They could tell that the question had offended her. Lwin was the object of affection of the village girls. Undoubtedly he was the worst person to have asked her the question.

This "no" had sent through the floor the last hopes of the two boys, who had done some advance planning.

The music and dancing were in full swing.

Lwin and his friend offered to pass out drinks and cigarettes in order to have an excuse to go everywhere, including the kitchen, which was the only place they hadn't been yet.

As they went through the crowd, they had to dodge invitations to dance. They quickly walked to the kitchen, a small building next to the house.

Lwin's heart pounded. His hands sweated and trembled. His voice was stuck in his throat.

They went in through a small door. There was very little light, just a diffuse reddish glow from the coals that had cooked the tamales and the soup. They had to squint in order to search in every corner.

When their hopes were about to be completely dashed, Lwin's sharp eyes spotted those two faces in the midst of the shadowy reddish kitchen. On the background of the black velvet night were outlined the faces of the two girls, lit by the brightness of the glowing coals.

They were pretending to watch a pot that was boiling for the midnight coffee.

The boys hadn't prepared themselves for starting a conversation and so they were left tongue tied by being caught off guard. The hopes of finding the women they were looking for had died like the fire, and when they suddenly found them, they didn't know what to say.

A plethora of ideas passed through their minds, reluctant to become words. They offered what they had in their hands to the surprised girls.

The girls hid their blushes in the napkins they were holding, at the same time saying "no" with a shake of their heads.

"Don't worry," said Lwin, "We've already asked your parents' permission to offer you this drink."

"That's not true," said one of the girls, "because my parents didn't come."

"But Malin's parents are here. They are also hosts of this party," put in the other boy.

"Thanks anyway. We don't drink," they said.

"It's okay that you turn down the liquor, but you won't dare turn down an invitation to dance," said Lwin rather spiritedly.

"There's no one to watch the coffee they're going to serve at midnight," said Malin, the host's sister.

"We admire you for being so hard-working, but on a night like this, you have to forget about working for a while," insisted Lwin's friend.

"We'll go ask permission and we if get it we'll be there soon. Go away for now because our parents might get upset at us for talking to you alone."

The two left the kitchen with the bottles in their hands. The music, the party, the entire atmosphere now looked rosier to the boys. Things had turned around and once again they found feeling and flavor in living this night, which they would have liked to make last a long time.

After a little while the two young women appeared with white *güipiles* that fell loosely over their patterned skirts, their hair braided with colored ribbon. They went to sit next to some women humming emotionally on their mats. Groups of boys focused their gaze on the corner where the girls were.

There was no music just then.

The old people spoke loudly, talking about things from the past. Some of the women began to sing and others to cry. They consoled one another.

On the rough table in front of the old people were gifts, mostly in the form of bottles. There was illegal liquor, beer and wine that had been brought by the guests. The owner of the new house called Lwin in front of the respected older men.

"We want you to open the bottle you brought and have a drink with us," they said.

Lwin enjoyed the respect of the villagers. He had reintegrated himself into the community, and once again gained their friendship and esteem.

He listened respectfully to the eulogies and advice of the men with hair whitened by the years.

He asked the host for permission to take wine to the women, a pretext to get near Malin. He went near her corner, serving the wine when the marimba broke into song once more, leaving the bottle with the group of women.

"Ma'am," he asked Malin's mother, "May I dance with your daughter?"

"I don't know if she wants to," answered the woman.

"May I have this dance?" he asked the girl.

She didn't answer. She stood up from her mat, rearranged

the necklace that adorned her neck, pulled two braids that were tied with bows to one side, and followed the boy as he went in among the people dancing the *son*.

At first, blushing under the gaze of others, her movements didn't quite fit the rhythm of the music. But after those first few moments she began to move rhythmically with the *son*. The pine needles under her feet were like rolling waves of the sea, taking her to a spiritual and mystic world. The braids on her chest moved with the rhythm of the dance. The feelings uncovered by the music were a juxtaposition of ideas and feelings matching the designs on the *güipil* and the *capixay*, wavy lines converging on the same spiritual apex, sharing the same spiritual plane, the beauty and the pain of life and the love that can not be translated fully into the symbols of the spoken language. One had to experience them in silence.

Lwin made his way through the people enjoying their modest entertainment. Now the crying began, as the tears fell. The subjects were always pain and sadness. The party continued on its course until it met the dawn.

Lwin and Malin spoke little. There are many things that don't need spoken language. This was the language of two hearts in love that transcended the borders of any language.

Lwin said good-bye before dawn. He had to leave the next day on a long trip.

"I'll find a way of seeing you," he said to Malin.

She didn't answer. Her heart began to feel great affection for that man.

By dawn the people were saying good-bye, one family at a time, as they left carrying sleeping children on their backs.

Many vendors came to town, loaded down with novelties of every type. Those from far away arrived in trucks, those from nearer by with mules straining under their loads. Hawkers arrived on foot, without mules, invisible under the large bundles wrapped in checkered cloth.

It would soon to be the fiesta in honor of the patron saint.

Mr. Diéguez, a mayor always eager for any activity promising extra income, had used various means to announce the upcoming fiesta. Both local people and outsiders were invited. It was necessary to disburse municipal funds to print posters, which were sent to all of the other mayors in the region: "Visit the Valley of Enchantment," they read, "Come and enjoy social, sports and religious events."

It was the third time that the mayor had fraudulently occupied the position. He managed to make politics his career, despite his limited schooling, for had completed only the third grade. But he had attached himself as a small fish to the big fish, and with his cooperativeness and gregarious spirit he had managed to climb up the ladder a few rungs. No one ever heard him express an original idea. His mind was a blank slate, and he always repeated what he was told.

That year it was to be a celebration with a new face. The Departmental Governor was to be invited to the opening ceremonies. Everyone was highly energized, working hard to save money for new clothes.

The vendors unveiled their wares in time. There were blue pants, wraparound skirts of cheap cotton, acrylic, or wool. There were dry goods of all prices and qualities. Mexican hats, costume jewelry, rings and earrings were on sale everywhere. Elsewhere there were leather articles: whips, sandals with eyelets and shoelaces, saddles, harnesses. There was a little bit of everything in the square.

The hawkers had taken over the town, corner by corner, street by street. They were in the arcades and corners of the buildings.

As the merchants arrived, their stalls were marked out on the plaza, and the highest bidders were given the best spots by the mayor's minions.

The children from the villages peeked curiously everywhere, anticipating the celebration. They looked out of the corners of their eyes as they passed baskets full of twisted rolls, fruit preserves, taffy wrapped in colored corn husks, cotton candy, bags of peanuts and all kinds of candies, making them imagine the fantastic flavors they had never enjoyed.

Joy was contagious. The children ran from one side to another amid the entangled, mildewed sheets which covered the square.

The children's attention was especially drawn to the mechanical rides that had come for the first time to that faraway Valley of Enchantment. There were merry-go-rounds that had little wooden horses with fixed eyes. A big ferris wheel began to go around like a big round November kite, bearing people away in a whirlwind. The flying chairs took the solid ground out from under their very feet, providing sensations they had never felt before. They thought that must be the sensation one felt in the metal birds that flew over their mountains.

A fortune-teller came in among the crowd with canaries and with parrots that said "bad words." The people formed a circle around the man, who gave out little pieces of colored paper to young and old anxious to know their future. The people laughed to hear the parrots speak. Couples consulted one another in whispers.

"Your fortune," yelled the man. "Fifteen centavos for a paper and ten centavos to read it," he announced. "Little bird, little bird, your luck has arrived, little bird," shouted one of the birds. The fiesta had not yet officially begun, but the fortune-teller was already fondling his earnings.

This year there would be two dance floors. One was in the large town meeting room, where there would be high society dances in suits, by special invitation only. Then there was a shed surrounded by wire mesh for the big dance for the Maya. On both dance floors there would be bars run by the local government.

The town hall was decorated with *pacaya* leaves, *patas de gallo* flowers, crepe paper in the mayor's favorite colors, and pine branches and needles.

Ten town deputies had been sent ahead of time to bring the decorations from the mountains. The mayor had decreed that one deputy from each village had to recruit twenty-five men for patrolling day and night all during the fiesta. Likewise he had to bring fifteen loads of dry firewood for the nightly bonfires.

According to the latest announcement, the inauguration of the fiesta would be Saturday. High Mass would be followed by a parade of the schoolchildren without their traditional hats or *capixayes*. They were to wear only the uniforms sold at the school.

Everything was ready. The food stands were smoking, the fat chickens showed their feet amid the slices of chayote and cabbage boiling in the large kettles. The tortilla makers applauded endlessly, kneeling in front of the griddles, poking the fire. The music from the jukeboxes beckoned potential customers, who crowded curiously around the entrances to the sawdust-carpeted bars.

"Mekel," Lotaxh said to her husband, who was resting in the entry way with his pants rolled up. He had just arrived from the cornfield.

"What?" he asked.

"It's almost time for the fiesta. You haven't thought about buying any clothes for the children. Especially for Lwin, who mentioned something a few days ago."

"What was that?"

"Well, for some time he's had his eye on a girl that he would like to have for a wife. He hadn't dared to tell us this, because he didn't want to cause us any financial problems. He was planning to ask us if he could get an advance contract to go work at the finca, so he would be able to buy some new clothes for the fiesta. Afterwards he would go work there, then when he came back we would go ask for the girl."

"Woman," answered Mekel, letting out a deep breath. "if I hadn't felt here in the depths of my soul the backbreaking work on the coast, if I hadn't experienced it in my own flesh as though it were just yesterday, the inhuman way they treat us there, if I didn't still feel the terrible climate in those uninhabitable places, I'd let Lwin go work there. But just thinking about it gives me chills and makes my flesh creep."

"If Lwin asks for money in advance, the contractor will give it to him right away. Lots of people are doing that these days. But the pay is now three times what it was, you know," continued Mekel.

"It's been exactly twenty-three years since I mortgaged our land title for the loan, which was the reason for my trip to the finca. Where is our land now? Who owns what was once ours?" he asked. "I signed some blank forms, and when we wanted to pay off the loan, the title was already registered in the name of that crook. No, Lwin should definitely not go anywhere," decided Mekel.

"If Lwin is interested in some girl, he should tell us about it. As far as the money is concerned, even if we have to work twice as hard, and scrape the bottom of the barrel to get the money together, we'll do it, but my son will never go to one of those places."

"The last few days I've been thinking about how we can buy clothes for the children and for ourselves. Tomorrow we can take our two fattened pigs to town real early. With the money we make we'll buy clothes for everyone, especially for Lwin. It's about time he got married. Lot of people are talking about that."

"Did he tell you what girl he's interested in?" Mekel was interested in knowing.

"Yes, we know her somewhat. She's the sister of the woman who just built the house. Her name is Malin. She's sixteen years old and is very respectful and hard-working," she concluded.

"How things change," commented her husband. "Remember when we got together we hadn't even met each other before. Our parents made the arrangements and we met one another on our wedding day. In a certain way, I'm glad he's making this decision."

"I don't think Lwin will forget our traditions," argued Lotaxh. "He's asking us to approve his plans, but if we don't like them, he'll surely go along with our suggestions."

"All right, we'll make a decision after consulting the diviner," said Mekel.

That same afternoon they threw the pigs down on the ground to check under their tongues, to be sure they didn't have mange. In fact, the animals were healthy.

It made Lotaxh sad to see those two beautiful animals being taken that early morning. She had become quite fond of them, the fruit of her work and effort. She had fattened them with great care.

"Ask whoever buys the pigs to save us a leg of the biggest one," Lotaxh asked her husband, as she watched them leave through the door of the hut.

They left at dawn so as not to be overtaken by the heat of the sun. By six o'clock they had arrived in town, with the fat oozing from the pigs' backs. The young men cooled off the pigs by throwing cold water on them.

They came to the place where the animals were sold. There were a lot of pigs, sheep, goats, birds, and they were offered very little.

"How much are you asking for your pigs, boy?" a man asked Mekel. "Hey, I think these animals are sick."

"No sir, my pigs don't have mange."

With one jerk, the man threw each of the animals down on the ground. He jabbed a stick down its muzzle, then he pulled its tongue out with both hands, like someone uprooting a cornstalk. He checked them and then kicked them so they would to get up.

The place was full of squealing animals.

"You can't see the mange, but the animals are sick," insisted the customer. "I'll give you twenty a head, which is a good price. Because if the authorities see you selling sick animals, not only will they take them away from you, but you'll also end up in jail."

Lwin, who had been silent until then, became irritated and blurted out:

"The pigs are healthy and we're not going to sell them for less than fifty each," he said, from the very start trying to avoid being tricked by the Ladino .

"You drive a harder bargain than your old man," answered the other.

"It's not that, Armín. I know you, because we went to school together. You ought to be more fair. Stop trying to trick people, man. We didn't steal these animals, it takes a lot of work to fatten them up."

"Okay, okay. Since we know each other I'll give you twenty-five for each animal and let's stop arguing."

After the haggling over the prices, looking for the point of equilibrium between supply and demand, which usually resulted to the disadvantage of the Maya, the pig buyer made his final offer:

"Neither you nor me: thirty eight for the larger one and twenty three for the other."

The next day they sent one of Lwin's brothers for the leg, which weighed ten pounds and which was made into tamales the very day of the fiesta.

The day the pigs were sold, the whole family had gone to town. Lotaxh arrived later with the small children.

Before leaving the house, she gathered up the savings that she had hidden at the bottom of the broken pot, in the gourd and in the armadillo shell. For months she had been saving the proceeds from the sale of pots, eggs and weavings. She wanted to buy herself a new *güipil*, for the one she had was torn and had faded trim. She tied her money up in a red handkerchief and set out with the children, with their freshly scrubbed faces.

The children were dressed in their least-mended clothes and put on a mask of happiness to go to town. They carried bags full of hope under their arms. Maybe their parents would buy them some clothes, or some sweets: there were so many different kinds, according to what they had heard. They would have a chance to see the mechanical rides, even if just to see how they worked. Those that slept, dreamt of all of this. Those that couldn't sleep, wished it would soon be morning.

When they got to town, they met Mekel and his two oldest children, who had gone on ahead with the pigs. They treated their taste buds to a glass of rice cooked in milk and a five-centavo *xheka* bun.

The children wanted to devour the fiesta with their eyes.

First they went to give the clothing stores the once over. They asked prices, took torso and leg measurements. They compared prices, whispered softly among themselves, made offers and bargained and then went to other stores.

By the second time around their string bags were swollen with four pants wrapped in old newspapers, and two silk *güipiles* with bright-colored trim. They still needed one more *güipil* and the wraparound skirts.

Mekel and Lotaxh had five children, three boys and two girls. By mid-morning the whole family had new clothes: pants, shirt and hat for the men; *güipil*, wraparound skirt, costume jewelry for the women. The money from the sale had been spent. Mekel resorted to the savings hidden in a bag tied into his long-sleeved underwear.

Lwin needed new clothes from head to toe. It would be an embarrassment to the family if he ran into Malin wearing old clothes for the town fiesta.

As the morning went on, it was becoming more and more difficult to make their way through the throngs that came to buy.

The family was carrying bundles full of sandals, clothing, oranges, *xhekas* and spices for the tamales. They tried to buy clothing in a little bit larger sizes. The children grew so fast by eating corn and greens.

They returned home at midday. They had to get the animals out of their corrals to take them to pasture. Only Lwin and his brother Nikol asked for permission to stay in town.

What remained of Lotaxh's savings had to come out of the red kerchief, leaving only a few centavos for something to eat. She didn't buy the *güipil* she had planned for. She was happier seeing her children happy, even if briefly. Their uncertain future always had her worried.

There were still two days until the start of the fair. Lwin and his brother roamed around wherever there were crowds. To tell the truth, Lwin had asked permission to stay, not so much for the noisy fiesta, but for the possibility of running into Malin. His brother knew this. They searched out all the corners. They tiptoed to look over the hats and heads of the crowds, but Malin was nowhere to be seen. The boy looked in each woman's face to see if it might be Malin's.

He soon tired of seeing so many faces coming up out of the centers of the *güipiles*. They were brown faces where intermittent, wavy, parallel lines converged. Dead-end roads lost in time, lingering hidden in the subconscious.

After walking quite a while, they ran into some friends from the village. They talked a while, and Lwin indirectly asked a couple of questions about Malin.

"What? You don't know where she went?" a friend who lived near her house asked in all seriousness.

"No, what happened?" asked Lwin in surprise.

"Just three days ago they left for the finca. The whole family went. I thought that you would have said good-bye to each another."

"No. There was no reason for that," he answered, feigning indifference. The news had fallen on him like a frightening *nawal* at midnight, turning his face pale, making his hands and feet tremble. He wanted to run off to some lonely place. He made a supreme effort to keep up a conversation with the group of young men.

When he took leave of his friends, the bearer of bad news slapped Lwin on the back. "Just kidding, relax. Get ready to dance with her tomorrow. The whole family is coming to see the parade," he said.

The group of boys enjoyed witnessing the discomfort they had caused Lwin. Nevertheless, he continued to pretend that he wasn't at all concerned about the matter.

In order to be allowed to attend the fiesta, Mekel's sons had to help feed the animals and shut them up in the corral. The parents would go only on the day of the Patron Saint to light some small candles to ask for his blessing, and to give thanks for the lives of their children.

At dawn on Saturday fireworks began to explode, long Roman candles that went up in the air, leaving behind streams of smoke, deafening people's ears. Then came High Mass, which the mayor and his family attended to ask for blessings and miracles in exchange for the Saint's new clothes they had donated.

Under a sky with patches of gray clouds, a multitude of school children, showing off their new uniforms, began to arrive. They shivered from the cold, missing their *capixayes*. They looked like newly-shorn sheep standing in a line in the cold, drizzly morning.

The Honorable Town Council marched at the head of the parade.

A few days before, in the last council meeting, the mayor had issued orders:

"We have to get our suits made, men. All the same color for the fiesta parade, because we're inviting the governor."

"What color, Your Honor?" asked the council members.

"Black. Black's a real good color," he said.

They walked along like a row of buzzards with their eyes bulging from the pressure of their ties. Behind, the interminable rows of schoolchildren. On the sidelines, behind the barricades, were more than forty thousand Maya, who had come down from all of the villages, hamlets and isolated areas. They had suspended their toil and allowed themselves a little respite to go to town. It happened once a year, not every day.

The mayor's opening speech lasted forty-five minutes.

"Neighbors of the Valley of Enchantment," began Diéguez. "On this historic day, on which we have assembled to recognize once more the blessings of our present government, blah, blah, blah ... and in the name of the Constitutional President of the Republic I hereby declare inaugurated the fiesta of our Patron Saint."

Finally, the mayor read a telegram from the governor, who was sorry he could not attend the inauguration: "I ask you to please give my most heartfelt greetings to our dear Indians, who I hope will enjoy their fiesta," he concluded.

The soccer field full of people resounded with applause. The unintelligible speech was finally over. By midday there was not enough room for all the people, who moved desperately from one side to another. They surged ahead by shoving and elbowing their way through the crowd. The children cried in desperation, feeling like they could hardly breathe.

It was very noisy with loudspeakers offering lottery tickets, jukeboxes going full blast, people shouting at the top of their lungs, foulmouthed parrots crying their insults. They enjoyed their annual fiesta with wall-to-wall people, something for which they had prepared very carefully.

Lwin had a hard time getting to where people surrounded the entrance to the church. His brother followed him and more people closed in behind them. Everyone wanted to see the Dance of the Conquest.

The monkey was the most zealous of the dancers, striking people with his double whip. He took charge of opening up a path so that the others could dance. He snapped his whip announcing to the public that he was coming through.

More than fifty policemen held back the crowd.

The tiger danced with an open maw; the deer danced with spellbinding horns, making people's heads spin. But it was the brandy with the "Deer" label that cast its spell over thousands and thousands of Maya, in whose minds danced barren illusions, briefly giving them a respite from reality, as they wandered all over town.

There danced the invader, that white man that had haunted Lwin ever since his childhood at home, at school, in the market. There he was, covered with mirrors, dazzling everyone with an impressive, aggressive look and character.

That must have been the one who conquered his ancestors Tekum Umam, Atanasio Tzul, Matalb'atz and many others. He was walking around, still carrying the sword in his hand with which he threatened thousands of frightened gazes in the shadow of the church. Babies clung tightly to their mothers' backs in view of that strange person.

Once more he was reasserting his power and authority over children, women and men, who stood with open mouths in admiration. This must be the one who imposed the laws on them and carried them out in accordance with his own wishes. The one who did not share power with anyone, not even with the majority, the one who mustered forces to compel respect. The one who directed the destiny of the Fatherland in the difficult areas of politics and economics. The one who allowed a few gaps in the so-called Constitution to keep the Mayas happy, keeping them immersed in their own culture, values, dress and languages, isolating them and keeping them away from the country's great ocean of riches. They were considered external things, impeding progress. The one who allowed them to amuse themselves with the trifles showcased to the world as Guatemala's colorful folklore.

Lwin's imagination was a bird that flew from branch to branch of the great tree of the national structure. Thinking of these things, he flew to a nearby branch: the parade that morning led by the Honorable Town Council, followed by thousands of miniaturized, minimized Maya disguised in Ladino clothing. They had been forbidden to use their *capixayes* to march past their people.

"Could it be," Lwin asked himself, "that to participate in national life we have to become Ladinos?"

Now he began to understand his father's questioning the *ajtzib'* about national identity. He didn't see his people at different levels of society. They weren't on the town council. They were the forty thousand admiring and applauding the parade of their own disguised children following the Ladino, who always led them as their light and their guide.

He kept flying into other branches and found no *capixayes* represented. He looked in vain in the top branches of the hierarchy, and found no one there either. He looked to see if there was anyone to the north, south, east or west. Then his imagination stumbled into one or two figures who looked like black moles on white Ladino faces. These had not only been disguised by changing their external appearance, but even worse, their organs of thinking and speaking had been emasculated. They would come out from their dark corners from time to time to pose for the isolated photographs of foreigners, and then sneak back once more into their corners. They never were permitted to come up with any ideas of their own. They were like the living dead, always being used by others. Their presence was exploited for the purposes of those who put them in a show case to be exhibited before the world, the great spectator. It was part of the benevolence of the law hiding under a mask of equality for all, but it really represented no one. They lived a sham life. But the hundreds of thousands that darkened the margins of the land and of the people, continued without representation.

"How many of us are there, really?" he asked his own conscience in a low voice.

"More than fifty per cent," he answered himself, putting a finger on his mouth as a signal to stay silent. "But they pretend," he continued, "that some day the country will be only made up of Ladinos. The rest of us will become part of it somehow, even if only by decree."

"But being Maya is an indelible seal," argued the voice of his conscience.

"Possibly, but you don't decide for yourself. There are third parties that decide for you."

His Mayan self asked again: "Does it depend on what you have, on what you wear, on what others decide for you, or does it depend on who you are and what you wear inside?"

He kept asking himself more questions.

That circle of space, full of mirrors, colors, marimba music and macabre figures that swirled by the wide eyes of the small children hidden on their mother's backs, was the entrance to the tunnel through which Lwin had fled to other dimensions.

That's where he was when the monkey's whip whizzed by, grazing the tip of his nose, bringing him back to the real world.

The police made superhuman efforts to contain the crowd, for everyone wanted to see.

"These mirrors continue to be a distraction for my people," Lwin complained. "When will they be able to touch more than mere mirrors?" He began to drift away again when his brother's voice interrupted him.

"Guess who I just saw," teased Nikol.

The man's imagination made his heart leap, as he squared off before his brother.

"Who?"

"Malin's parents," he answered, leaving a lingering doubt by his phrasing, in order to make his brother suffer.

"What about them?" he asked. His hands were sweating and his heart raced.

"I saw them heading toward the food stands. They were with some other people from the village."

Seizing his brother by the shoulders and shaking him, he asked the same question: "Did you see her or not?"

"Yeah, man, she was there, too, it's no big deal," he protested.

Lwin let out an almost imperceptible sigh. The image of the woman he loved, that face with the look of innocence and of the ages, like the patterned countenance of his people, was his motive for being there, using the fiesta as a pretext.

The word for love in other languages could not be translated faithfully into Lwin's personal language. It had come late and mystically into his heart. They were indecipherable feelings that didn't need sound or sign to be communicated. Lwin's spirit was completely and absolutely possessed by that feminine creature. It was a story of two people in love who speak no human language, but are in constant and permanent communication on the level of the spirit and of the heart.

Moved by that invisible force, he made his way like a ship through a great sea of people, leaving behind him a wake of protests in the crowd.

He went in the indicated direction. His brother tried to reach him, but got stuck among a group of vendors, and preferred to let him go on.

From afar, Lwin managed to see Malin's father. They were close to the fortune teller. He didn't know whether to come near or to wait for a little while. But an inner impulse kept pushing him forward.

He arrived just as Malin's father was getting her fortune told. He came near them, took off his hat and greeted them. To Malin and her sister he cast a sweet glance. She pulled at the hem of her *güipil*, trying to hide her blushing at having been discovered getting her fortune told.

He didn't interrupt any further, and stood watching the canaries perform. The owner spun a wheel with colored pieces of paper, put the one intended for young ladies in front of one of the birds and spoke up loudly: "Here canary, little canary. Take out the fortune in the paper." The beautiful bird first sang inside his colorful cage and then stuck his head out the door. With four pecks, he took out four little pieces of colored paper.

"That'll be ten centavos for each paper and ten to read all four," said the man.

"We'll get them read later," answered don Matin Anton.

After paying their forty centavos, they went to talk where there were fewer people passing by.

Malin was beautiful. It was a natural beauty, without any artificial intervention, and was more a reflection of an inner state than of an outer ostentation. She wore a wraparound skirt with animal designs on a dark marbled background. The long white *güipil* came down over her knees. Down her back hung a couple of braids interwoven with a rainbow of ribbons. It was loosely rolled down, and ended in two knots like roses in full bloom. Around her head, sprouting like a corn shoot, circled ten furrows of dazzling necklaces framing her dark face.

Lwin's words came out impulsively. At times his tongue was tied. He invited the family to some rice pudding and *xhekas*. He walked around with them a long time, but to him it seemed extremely short, and finally he said good-bye.

"Are you coming tomorrow, don Matin?" he asked.

"We don't know yet. If the women aren't too tired to walk, maybe we'll come. Right now we're going home because we left three small children there."

"Very well, have a good trip. I'm going back soon. I just need to find my brother, who should be here somewhere in the crowd," he said. "Tomorrow there will be a dance. I hope you'll come," he suggested.

They had come asking for Malin's hand in marriage on three occasions, but each time Matin had refused to receive the parents of the suitors.

Malin was anxious to get home that afternoon. She wanted to know what the little papers said, since her future depended on it. She really liked Lwin, but that wasn't reason enough to marry him.

When she got home, she ran to look for her brother, who could read. She took him to her father so that she could ask the boy to read the papers.

They sat at the entrance to the hut, clustered around the boy, who deciphered the papers one by one.

They came to the following respective conclusions:

The green paper referred to health. It predicted that the good health that Malin was currently enjoying might be greatly affected by a serious illness in the near future. She should be very careful not to get sick.

The yellow paper referred to business and money. It said that the stars were exercising a favorable influence on her. Shortly there would be a great opportunity to earn some extra income. Only, there was a shadow on her path, a person who wanted to harm her, and that is why several projects of hers had failed. The little paper also suggested that she pass a black hen over all her body and then go and spill the bird's blood and leave its body lying at the crossroads along with a bunch of luckynut leaves, rue and a handful of black salt. All of this would chase away the dark shadows hovering over her life.

She didn't attach much importance to what she had heard; what she wanted to hear was the prediction about love. Two papers remained and she was obviously nervous.

"Read another one," she asked, practically begging her brother.

"Work hard and unceasingly, while you still have youth and energy," said the brown one. "Follow the example of the ant, that stores up food in good times and so isn't hungry in times of scarcity. Work and savings are the two roads that will lead you to eventual success."

"Work! For us there is work day and night, from the time we're born until the time we die. Nothing but work and more work," she commented. "We go through life sprinkling the face of the earth with our sweat, until we are squeezed dry like a sponge and we never manage to rise above the subhuman life in which we find ourselves," she finished in anger.

One little paper remained, which had lost her interest somewhat, because of the emotions provoked by the previous one.

"Dear friend," it began. "You have many suitors. You are at the most critical crossroads of your life. You can choose what strikes your fancy, but remember that you should do this with God's help and your parents' advice. Because of all the men coming around, only one will make you happy. Remember that the true value of people is not in externals, nor in riches or physical appearance. All of this ends and has a limit. The value of a man is in his sentiments and what he carries inside of him. Be of good courage and go forward," ended the writing on the pink paper.

That afternoon Lwin and his brother stayed, entertained by the different festivities. Around four in the afternoon the great inaugural ball began in the town hall. According to the mayor's instructions, the Maya weren't allowed in, only the Ladinos arriving in full dress. The two boys watched from the windows guarded by police with batons and whips. The people jammed in front of the windows. Diéguez came in with his retinue, the sale of tickets stopping as the town boss passed by.

Taking advantage of the confusion in this large group of people, a pair of Maya managed to slip in and sit down on some benches in the hall. There were new tables spread out everywhere, displaying various brands of hard liquor in bottles, intended to liven up the atmosphere. In the middle of the hall the mayor, his face red from the liquor he had begun drinking from early on, spun with his partner in ever larger concentric circles. The people made way for him and greeted him. Faces wrinkled up under the influence of the liquor. The music resounded in the large hall adorned with pine needles and *pacaya* leaves. The Mayan couple was infected by the gaiety of the event, and after a while they came out of their corner to try to dance in their own way.

They had enjoyed the dance for no more than two minutes when four policemen fell upon them. The man wanted to resist, but it was useless. They threw him out the door with shoves and kicks, and he fell on his face onto the cobbled street. Later he was taken to jail, which was starting to fill up at about that time.

The brothers looking through the window left when they

saw what had happened, and went back to their own village as evening was falling.

The Patron Saint's day dawned, the principal day of the fiesta, a fresh-faced morning. There was a festival of clouds in the sky, many fluffy clouds turning into scattered gold dust in the rays of the rising sun.

Mekel's family got up early to feed the sheep, chickens and pigs, so they could go enjoy the fiesta. The children were cheery as they went about their chores, thinking about the bits of happiness that came their way once or twice a year.

Looking at what was left of their savings, they confirmed the fact that the armadillo shell, the old jars and the knotted handkerchiefs were empty. Not a single coin remained. They took what they could find on hand to sell and earn a few centavos.

They loaded the mule up with dry firewood, wrapped the chicken eggs in corn husks and put them in the bag, as well as part of the year's bean supply. From their one old stained chest, they took the new clothes they were to put on out of the newspapers in which they were wrapped.

No one went without something new. They walked toward the town, carrying their joy on their faces. They greeted their acquaintances and friends, who were also going in search of the fiesta.

Lwin walked along with his parents. The children ran ahead and behind. Sometimes they disappeared around bends in the trail, but soon reappeared, spilling out onto the path.

"We should go get your fortune told," Lotaxh told her son.

"Yes, mother."

"Your father is thinking of inviting don Matin for a drink."

"Yes, mother."

Lwin was deep in thought and paid scant attention to Lotaxh's words. He, too, was making plans.

From the ridge where they could see the town, they could see people coming from everywhere, like army ants in May.

That morning the little villages hanging on the pillar-like hills had been emptied. In blue pants and squeaky sandals they needed the distraction of jumping to the notes of a *son* and drinking some brandy that would scrape their throats on its way down. This didn't happen every day; it was just once a year.

The smoke from the food stands hung over the town. It looked like a big blue lake on a still wind.

Mekel and his family wanted to offer their merchandise for whatever they could get. But it was a festive time, and no one wanted to buy anything but special treats.

They soon arrived at the center of the town, where the people milled around elbowing each other, stepping on one another with their new sandals, pushing and shoving. Children got separated from their parents. Boyfriends and girlfriends could touch one another. The women selling gruel held on to their steaming pots and the vendors shouted at the people face to face.

The canary and parrot cages had been reinforced with poles stuck into the ground, so they would not be dragged away by the sea of people.

One of the parrots was constantly being bumped into, and seeing so many people, he shouted insults to the wind. "Bug off, you bitch." he said as he tumbled around in his cage.

The people laughed to see the birds talk, although few understood Spanish.

"I want to have my fortune told," said Lwin to the bird man.

"Are you married or single?"

"Single."

He twirled the container and the parrot managed to pull a bundle of papers out with his beak. He put it in his master's hands at the same time as he squeezed the elastic folds of his eyes in slow motion and cocked his head to one side to watch a buzzard pass through the sky.

"Fifty centavos. Shall I read it for you?"

"No, another one for my sister."

"She's single, right?"

"Yes."

"It's my turn!" shouted the other parrot, which had begun to shed some feathers.

The children's dream of riding little wooden horses on a merry-go-round finally came true. They got off like dazed little chickens with air in their heads. One of them vomited on his blue pants, for he'd never felt the earth move beneath his feet. They were dizzy and they had to be bought a red-colored drink.

Curiosity bulged in the eyes of young and old alike. The family tried to visit most of the places, so that the children would have fun.

After going excitedly through the fair, they decided to visit the dance hall, the one for the Maya, surrounded by wire mesh. Mekel was at the head of the line and paid for everyone, all having their right wrist stamped with the town seal so they could enter the hall.

Lwin whispered something in his father's ear. They opened up a breach among the people until they came to where Malin was standing with her parents, brothers and sisters, pretending it was by chance. They greeted one another, and made some comment about the fiesta. The heat was unbearable, with the people all squeezed together.

The music awakened people's emotions. It was a shared collective sentiment, a shared delight, a shared nostalgia. The notes of the marimba narrated that same history of the Maya people.

Mekel, followed by his wife, went to mix among those that were dancing, dripping with sweat. The couple made their way through the whirling *güipiles* and *capixayes*, and strengthened by their emotions, began to dance.

Couples danced, man and woman face to face, forgetting

space and time.

After the first few numbers, they looked for Malin's parents to have a drink together, warm up their stomachs and relax their muscles.

Then they continued dancing, motivated by the sorrows that came out of the depths of the music. It was partly happiness and pain, sorrow and anger, peace and confusion.

The paradox between the material and metaphysical world manifested itself in the hearts of the people. They were caught in between the past and the present.

Everyone vibrated in harmony with the music. Malin moved rhythmically in front of Lwin. In her mystical world, green, yellow, and pink papers marched along, attached to canary beaks warbling like the marimba music in their ears. She would have liked to capture the moment and lock it in a cage where it would never die. Her heart beat anxiously under the white silk *güipil* which wrapped her woman's body. She stood erect like a lily of the field, he like a mountain goat seeking love with all of the strength nature had granted him. The rapture of two spirits fused into one quickly opened the path to love: a pure, natural and profoundly human love.

Outside, the fiesta had reached its culmination. There was no spot that was not in motion: the wheels, the women inside the food stands serving steaming tamales out of the clay trays, wrapped in green leaves. The dancers never stopped spinning around in circles. People milled around and moved from one place to another, looking for fun. The police carried drunks off to an already packed jail. And now money was leaving the last knots of the handkerchiefs.

"Come on in," shouted the women. "There's *pepián*, pork tamales, red beans with fried pork rinds. Come on in, folks, come on in. We have *súchiles*, *chilate*, and *pinol* to drink." Everything moved with a deafening noise.

Only Mr. Diéguez was motionless, flat on his back in bed with clusters of flies on his drooling mouth.

"Somebody's knocking on the door, Juana. Go see who it is," ordered the mayor's wife.

"In a minute the maid returned: "Doña Coronada, they're looking for the mayor. A lady says he's her *compadre*."

"Tell her to come in, it must be Lencha."

"Please come in, Doña Coronada is in the kitchen."

"Thanks, Juana."

"Come in, *comadre*, come in! Don't just stand there in the doorway, after all you're family."

"Thank you so much. Well, here I am. How are you this morning? How's your husband? Here's a pound cake I brought you."

"Oh, thank you so much, *comadre*, you shouldn't have bothered. The old man is sleeping it off, you know how he is, especially at times like this. Usually he spends it drinking. That's how he is, *comadre*. I hardly pay attention any more."

The two women continued talking until afternoon, raking all the neighbors over the coals.

While the crowd was still enjoying the festivities, a convoy of five military trucks arrived without being noticed by the populace. The trucks were full of soldiers.

The purpose was to shanghai young men into military service, taking advantage of the crowd of rural folk at the fiesta. The officer in charge ordered the trucks to be left outside town, so they could surround the area and trap the largest number of men possible.

Soon the news spread everywhere: soldiers! the quota! the army! the service! Every man for himself! The news was passed from mouth to mouth throughout a sea of people that stampeded loaded down with fear.

They tore down the doors of the dance hall; the wire mesh was left bloody from the desperate hands that had grabbed it. Bunches of women's hair were left entangled on the wires.

The monkey's mask was broken, for there had not been enough time to take it off. The monkey had been squashed by the crowd. The tiger was like an anguished soul, his tail trailing behind him, as he gulped the wind with an open maw.

The annual joy froze on the peasants' faces. The fiesta was only half over, one more blow to those lives.

Everywhere there were hats thrown down, clay pots broken, tamales gutted, bottles smashed to bits, sandals torn off and looking for their owner's feet, children lost, women with disheveled hair, and men struggling with the soldiers.

A sound like an earthquake could be heard as the earth responded to the trample of panic-stricken people rushing toward the ravines, over the roads and paths, up through the folds in the mountains. They tried to find their way back to their villages, left empty up on the high ridges, all regretting they had come to look for festive joy.

They had come down for a bit of relaxation and amusement. They returned silent, defeated, anguished, cut off from family members, no longer physically and spiritually whole.

Those who had come down smiling that morning with their children, now returned gaunt under the weight of their pain.

In his flight, Lwin, pursued by two soldiers of his own people, passed by where the fortune-telling birds had been, and in a lightning glance managed to see the crushed cages. The beautiful feathers were mixed with blood and mud. The parrot with his beak half open was probably uttering his last curse. The owner had his head between his hands, profusely shedding tears.

Lwin forged ahead, the two soldiers behind. They were running at the same speed at first, but Lwin was slowing down. Three hundred feet, a hundred, twenty-five, ten, until one of them seized a sleeve of Lwin's *capixay*. When he realized he was caught, Lwin made a heroic effort, and yanked with all of his strength. The sleeve came off in the hands of the soldier, who tripped on a stone and fell staggering to the ground. In his left hand Lwin carried his new hat, the one he had just worn for the first time. The other soldier tried to trap him in an alley between moss-covered adobe walls. There was nowhere to go and his only chance was to jump the wall. On the first try he fell and came sliding down the damp wall. On a second try he threw the hat to the other side and grabbed the wall with both hands. Just as Lwin was leaping to the other side, the soldier jumped up to reach him, but managed only to touch the edge of his sandal. Unable to sustain his weight, Lwin slipped on some stones and fell among human waste.

He had some difficulty making his way through the corn and *chilacayote* plants. The pain in his knee kept him from continuing his flight. Instead, he crouched among the dense leaves.

"Find that bastard. He must be here," said one of them.

"Wouldn't it be better to go around the wall to see where he could've gone?" suggested the other. "You go on this side and I'll go on the other."

"Be careful, it's full of crap everywhere."

They were clueless about where Lwin might have escaped to. They went looking for him among the bushes, stabbing their bayonets every which way, but found no one.

Lwin's nose was just inches away from one of the soldier's boots. It smelled of dung, and he held his breath.

"We better go," said one of them, who was still holding the sleeve of the *capixay*.

They went back the way they had come, carrying the sleeve as a claim ticket, like a human arm without its owner. The trucks were filling up with men, tied up and under heavy guard. One of Lwin's brothers, who was about eighteen, had been caught and was in the second truck parked in front of the town hall.

Once night had fallen, Lwin managed to come out of his hiding place. He climbed over a stone promontory and taking a circuitous route, headed up toward his village, where he arrived after midnight. He walked very slowly on account of the pain in his knee. He went by his house to get a blanket and to bring the news about his brother that was like a sword piercing the family's heart. Then he went up into the rocky hills to hide for the two days that the soldiers would still be in town.

In the cave of Yulch'en he met men from various villages. They took turns going to one of the villages for food. Five more trucks had arrived in town to take away the men who were being chosen.

"The lame, the deaf-mutes, the stutterers, those with only one eye and those with any other physical or mental handicap, have them stand to one side," ordered the commander.

Since there was no doctor there, the town authorities issued the documents exempting those with some disability. People filled the mayor's house day and night. Women and men over fifty years of age stood in line to ask for exemptions.

There were lots of certificates for the disabled. Parents, wives, and relatives begged, cried, offered money and animals, anything in exchange for the freedom of their family members. Many were exempted, but many others were mustered in to receive training at one of the country's military bases.

The hunting down of frightened men had lasted three days in the area, sowing fear and pain. It was three days of insomnia and sudden unpleasantness, hiding in the depths of dark caverns. Three days of going and coming to town to beg and even kneel before those who would decide their destiny.

"Why do we have to run, hide as though we were criminals, and sneak around through ravines and caves?" wondered a group of men wrapped in their blankets around the fire that dispelled the fear inside the cave.

"What are they taking men to the army for, Lwin?" asked one of the men.

"I think they are going to defend what they call the Fatherland. The Ladino's Fatherland," he said.

181

"But what is "fatherland," any way? I could never really understand the meaning of that word during the few years I spent in school," he continued. "I learned to sing the national anthem, I learned about symbols and a few other things, but what do they really mean by "fatherland"? Whose is it and why does it exist?" asked the youth, interested in expanding his knowledge of all of that.

"All the citizens of a country," spoke up Lwin, "are supposed to have certain rights and responsibilities. This is true just about everywhere in the world, although in some cases they may limit people's rights or put obstacles in their way. It ought to be that way here too, but in practice, it isn't."

"As in most aspects of national life, the Maya and the peasants get the short end of the stick. When it's a question of responsibilities, they remember us. But when it comes to rights, we're the last ones to receive the benefits."

"The whole legal system is unjust right from the start, from the time the laws are passed until they are enforced with arbitrariness and partiality. They don't worry about us, the majority of the citizens."

"But Lwin, if as you say" continued another, "patriotism is a collective value of all the citizens, don't you think that children of Maya and Ladinos of all social classes should convince themselves they should defend this nation of ours?"

"That's how it should be," answered Lwin. "But there's more to it than that. If we were given the opportunity to understand what having a fatherland means, they wouldn't have to come and pursue us like wild animals, trampling on our human dignity."

The barking of dogs in the village at the foot of the cliffs, brought a halt to the conversation. There were lights among the houses. The soldiers were probably searching for them.

At 9:00 o'clock in the morning of the fifth day, the trucks full of well-guarded men started up their motors.

The departure began in front of the people, mainly adult

men and women, who cried in silence.

Those that undertook the journey said good-bye as though they would never come back. Those that stayed behind remained attached to their own flood of tears, hands stretched out to emptiness like trying to catch a butterfly escaping from their fingers.

Lotaxh stood next to her daughter, watching her son waving his hand good-bye as he left.

"Take care of yourself," mouthed the mother in soundless words.

Matin Tikxhun, the boy who had been with Lwin all through elementary school, had continued his studies in the city. He had kept his promise to Lwin when they had said good-bye that wet winter day long ago.

Using the books he was sent, Lwin was able to continue studying various subjects. Afternoons when he returned from working in the fields he devoted himself to studying, trying to analyze and compare each idea, each author's point of view and draw his own conclusions concerning various aspects of society and national life.

By now he managed to maintain contact and communication with various people from town as well as former schoolmates, some missionaries who arrived occasionally and various specialists to exchange views on social problems. One of his goals was to ascertain the true cause of the Ladino-Maya dichotomy, desiring to build a bridge of understanding that would permit an encounter leading to true development.

One day when a social scientist arrived at a hamlet near Jolomk'u to carry out some research, Lwin realized that his people invariably reacted differently to strangers. A heritage of distrust had remained in them as a result of so much trickery and abuse.

These situations motivated Lwin to study the behavior and variety of Ladino reactions, discovering many explanations for things he wondered about.

Talking one morning with a Ladino friend, he offered an opinion:

"I think it's a question of attitudes and will, more than events of the past," said Lwin. "We have to find the positive aspects of the two cultures, and utilize them, in order to build a new society that will permit everyone to have access to well-being."

"Yes, Lwin," answered the friend. "Because until now our environment has been full of the prejudices of one against another, because of bad experiences. This good will of which you are speaking has to come from both sides, because I must emphasize that not all of us Ladinos are oppressors of your people. There are a lot of us that don't make those kinds of distinctions. It's also true that there are many Ladinos that share your economically and educationally disadvantaged situation."

"Friend, in most homes in the towns and the cities, there is at least one of my people working as a domestic, doing the heaviest housework. We should recognize that on occasion they are treated with dignity, but in many other cases they are treated with disdain and humiliation. They are exploited and underpaid. They don't receive the benefits they are legally entitled to nor the respect they deserve as human beings. There is the widespread false notion that because up here in our distant mountain villages we lack job opportunities, education and training, and are so needy, we have to accept as a bountiful gift whatever the employers deign to pay us in exchange for our services."

"Unfortunately," replied the friend, "there are a lot of cases of forced marginality, but I'm pleased to tell you that there are also some good Ladinos who have helped your people.

Right now I know some who altruistically fund the education of Maya students, or who have helped victims of the violence: orphans or widows left with many children. Social scientists are working to find solutions in different areas. There are families that share their lives and wealth with the Maya without discrimination."

"I hope some day," concluded Lwin, "we can establish objectives and common goals for equal opportunity, without some superior to others, and work together for progress."

Lwin and his parents were the only ones at home. The rest of the family had gone to the countryside.

"Son, your mother and I have been doing a lot of thinking, and have waited until now to discuss things with you and make a joint decision," said Mekel. "As you know, most young men marry before they're twenty. We think that it's time you thought about choosing some girl to be your wife."

"Yes, Lwin," added his mother. "We would like for things to be done the traditional way. That is, if you have a girl in mind, we'd be glad to go ask permission for you to marry her. We don't want you to elope, because there might be problems later on. There are some girls in this village who are very hard-working and respectful, or in other villages, if you prefer."

"I'm not quite sure what to say," answered Lwin. "We're so poor. I don't want to cause any financial problems. To go and ask for a girl means spending money and we have no place to get the money from. Yes, it's true there's a young lady that has interested me for some months now, but I want your opinion of her," he said.

"Who is it?" asked Mekel, the only one not fully clued in on the matter. Lotaxh knew Malin very well and liked her.

"Malin, the daughter of don Matin Anton," replied Lwin, his heart contracting as he spoke the name that had become an obsession with him. "If you give me permission, I'll elope with her," he suggested.

"Oh!" said Mekel. "I don't know the family too well, but I believe they are hard-working people and the few times I've seen the girl, she's seemed to me to be very respectful, unassuming, and hard-working, just like her mother, who greets us on the street whenever we see her. How old is she?" he asked.

"She's sixteen," answered Lotaxh. "The day they dedicated her sister's house, I was able to get some information about her from acquaintances, and they gave me very good reports on her. We have to hurry and make the arrangements," continued Lwin's mother, "if our son makes this decision, because I've heard that there are some other young men courting her, and they might beat us to it," she concluded.

"Have you already talked to her, son?" asked Mekel.

"About this, not much. We've danced a few times."

"Good, the first thing we need to do is go visit the diviner to get his advice. There's one thing I can't agree to, and that's your eloping with her, because that causes trouble between families. Don't worry about the expenses. We'll see if we can get a loan or we'll sell something."

"We should go to the diviner today," said Lotaxh, "I forgot to tell you that a neighbor told me that Matin Anton's family is thinking of traveling to the fincas after the fiesta."

A sad-looking diviner predicted for them that black clouds were nearing Jolomk'u and all the villages scattered among the mountains and valleys of the region. Peace, like the tranquil waters of those places, would shortly be disturbed by catastrophes. The race of the dispossessed and forgotten would suffer the consequences of those catastrophes.

"Now, about the girl you mentioned," said the old man, "she's a flower among the rocks, with a troubled heart at the crossroads of life. She doesn't know which way to go. I see that she's about to take flight like a white dove and lose herself in the infinite blue of the sky. You must realize this and hurry to capture her innocent heart. Signals from my right side tell me that God has created one for the other and that they will achieve that peace and tranquility which are the sources of happiness," he decided. "Light your candles, go to the sacred ancestral places to ask for their help. B'en is coming soon, an appropriate day for making marriage proposals. And go in the company of the elders of the family."

A few days later, Lotaxh began the preparations for the proposal with enthusiasm. The grinding stones crushed the kernels of corn with cacao, sapodilla seeds, and black pepper. The women dusted off the net bags hanging in the corners, full of gourd cups to be used for the sacred drinks.

The elders, weighed down with the years, arrived the same time as B'en. They were the ones in charge of facilitating the dialogue with their language full of the accumulated experience and eloquence appropriate for these supremely important occasions in the life of the younger generation.

The night was erasing the last traces of the day. On his back Mekel carried a pot of *chilate*, a pot born at the dawn of the culture of a people that had lost the memory of themselves down through the paths of time.

Two older couples walked in a shaky fashion, feeling out the road. They were followed by Mekel and his wife, who were following in the footsteps of those who had sculpted life in stones, those who once lived in Xib'alb'a, who forged their identity from beyond the other end of the umbilical cord of history. They walked one behind the another in the direction of Malin's house.

"Hello there!"

There were no dogs at home. They had taken off in pursuit of a bitch in heat.

Someone with lighted pitch pine came out of the only door of the hut.

"Who is it?"

"It's us, don Matin," said one of the grandparents. "We came to ask you for permission to come in and partake of the sacred drink that we bring you."

"What do you want? Why are you out wasting your time at this hour of the night?"

"Yes, sir, we have disturbed your rest, but as you know, this is our custom, and we should continue the tradition of our elders. We are asking you for permission to talk a while. Our son Lwin has his eye on your daughter, which is why we came to bother you."

"I don't have any time. The girl isn't thinking of getting married, and besides, my family will soon be traveling far away. So please go home."

"Sir, be so kind. We just want to chat with you and your wife for a bit, so please accept our modest gift."

"I can't accept anything. That would be like making some kind of commitment, so you better go home. It's useless to insist. I can't afford to repay you for your drink, I'm poor," said Matin, visibly annoyed.

"That's not important," insisted the elders standing in front of the house. "What we ask of you is that you at least accept the gift, because Mother Corn could be offended, and this could result in unfortunate consequences for our children," observed one of the grandfathers, bolstering his argument with a cultural value.

One of the old women sat down on some firewood. She was tired.

"It's impossible," said Matin Anton, "if you want, come back another day. I'll consult with my family. You should tell me what day you're coming, because I'm very busy and sometimes I'm not home," he said.

"That's all right, don Matin," said the one in charge. "We'll come back at this same time three days from now."

According to cultural norms, dialogue is never established on the first occasion. Having agreed to receive them on a subsequent visit augured well for the retinue.

Mekel put down the pot with the sacred drink and left it on the threshold. Matin insisted he would not accept it, but after a long conversation the pot stayed there.

"It's all right, you can leave it there, just out of respect for the old ladies that are with you and the lateness of the hour," said the head of the house.

It was the middle of the night by the time the group returned home.

Matin Anton's behavior had been correct. It couldn't be considered rudeness under these circumstances. If he had allowed the visitors in, it would have been a demonstration of weakness on his part and dishonor for his family.

Three days later, they came once more to Malin's house. She had gone to visit a sister, so as to not be present at the event. They were invited in and sat on some benches. Only Malin's parents and the elder brother were there.

"Don Matin, doña Torol, with your permission we'd like to use your fire to prepare some gruel," said the eldest man.

Lotaxh immediately put a jar of water on the hearth stones and began to blow on the fire. When the water boiled, she prepared for each one present a gourd of black corn gruel with the corn dough she had taken out of the pot. Meanwhile they talked about routine things: corn, work in the field, the first rains, animals.

When the corn drink was finished, Mekel approached the eldest of his family and, taking a bottle out of his bag, gave it to him. The latter stood up and spoke in the following manner:

"This is the product of the spirits; this is the spirit of our ancestors. Let us eat and drink to alleviate today's fatigue and relax our minds." He removed the corncob stopper from the mouth of the bottle and made a mark for each person, who drank the contents with furrowed brow, then spat.

They wiped off the mouth of the bottle with their elbows and then passed it to their neighbor, who repeated the action.

The conversation rose above the cigarette smoke, sustained by the clever tongues of the elders, before getting into the main subject. The rough hands of the peasants amused themselves by caressing the smooth texture of the gourd cups.

Soon the one in charge focused the conversation directly on the reason for the visit.

"Sir, madam, we must remember that it has been predestined by the infinite wisdom of Our Father God, that men and women each seek their own mate for the purpose of perpetuating the seed of humanity on Mother Earth," he began. "So it has been since remote times. This has been the custom since the dawn of the world. Our lives are a product of this natural process, which we must pass on to succeeding generations. In fulfillment of this destiny and out of the respect we have toward each other, we humbly come before you to tell you that our son Lwin has centered his heart and his feelings on the heart of your daughter Malin. We have consulted the will of Our Father God by means of the diviner, and it is his will that these two young people unite their lives for the honor of our family and the glory of our race," he concluded.

"For our part, ladies and gentlemen" spoke up a feminine voice. "we support the wholesome intentions of our grandchild. We have come to assume our responsibilities toward you, so that their life together can follow the commandments of our parents. It would be a great honor for us if your daughter were to become be a part of our family."

As the older men and women took turns at persuasion, Mekel urged drinks on people to lighten their imaginations and their bodies.

"God knows," intervened Lotaxh, "that we lack many material things, that we have no wealth, and that our lives depend on the effort of our daily work. We can give but little on account of our poverty, but we give you the key to our hearts, which beat full of love, understanding and solidarity.

We ordinarily share this with everyone, so, even more so, we are going to see to it that your daughter becomes a full-fledged member of our family.

We promise you she won't lack for food, clothes, grinding stone, pots, colander, water jar or a few centavos to take to the market," she declared in an emotion-laden voice.

Malin's grandfather who had arrived late, spoke up:

"Both the man and the woman, according to our traditions, must fulfill certain requirements in order to be able to take on a responsibility of this nature," he began. "Certainly no man or woman is capable of attaining perfection, but, if possible, they should try to free themselves from the heavy burdens that oppress the human spirit. In the name of our family I thank you, who have taken notice of our daughter Malin, but we're sorry to have to tell you that ..."

His cough had cut off his message. A certain nervousness arose among those present.

A swallow of brandy cleared up the old man's cough. He was sweating from the effort of coughing.

"We must tell you," he began again, "that we can't give you an answer at this time. We need to find out how the girl feels and have to consult the other members of the family and get the advice of our diviner. You mustn't waste your time coming again," he said to Malin's father. "We'll answer you when we see you in town, and we don't want you to go to any more expense."

"Not at all, don Matin," said Mekel. "It's our responsibility to come for the answer. It's a serious matter, and it can't be resolved on the street or on the square. God willing, we'll be here within a week for some favorable news," he said.

The night was as dense as black obsidian. Only the penetrating eyes of the villagers, accustomed to the dark, could make out the winding trails hidden in the brush. They walked on a sea of hopes, no longer feeling the day's fatigue.

Lwin and another friend were waiting near Malin's house.

The boy whistled a melancholy lover's tune, the same tune the marimba had played the first time he danced with Malin.

Matin Anton's relatives were gathered for a family council: grandparents, uncles, older brothers and Malin. A number of suitors had come earlier and showed their interest in marrying her. Each one of the marriage proposals of the suitors and their families was analyzed in front of Malin to ask her opinion.

"I leave the selection of my future husband up to your judgment," she declared." You know that ever since I began to think about my life, I've tried to follow your advice, and I've always tried to respect and obey you. I think this time you will also want the best for me, as you have always done."

As the names of each of the three young men were mentioned, she indicated her disapproval in some fashion.

She was seated next to her mother, near an aunt who was her confidant. When Lwin's name was mentioned, she blushed and bowed her head without saying anything.

The family made the decision to stop visits from families other than Mekel's.

They gave Malin much advice, many recommendations and explanations about a woman's role in family life: respect for the husband, care of the children, housework, acceptance of poverty and other suffering.

When the week was over, the contingent of Lwin's relatives arrived for the third time to Malin's house, just as night was falling. This time Lwin came with a big bundle of bread, chocolate, meat and brandy.

Malin's relatives were waiting for them. They were courteously received and invited inside the house. Only the adults were present, the children having been sent to bed. Malin was sitting on her little mat, next to the women of her family.

The elders had employed the most convincing words to gain favorable decision on this third occasion.

Lwin sat opposite Malin. He could see her directly without effort. Her head was bowed, listening to the men speak. Even though her mind and heart were invaded by uncertainly, she felt pulled by the boy's magnetism.

The spokesman for the hosts went into a long discourse on the responsibilities of a man and his wife, of the procreation of children, of conserving the great values of the culture, of mutual respect between the family and the local community.

Then the conversation took a friendly turn and headed directly toward approval of the proposal by the girl's relatives.

There was a supper offered by the hosts, and when the third proposal visit was over, they fixed the date for the ceremony of the gift of firewood and for the concert, which is tantamount to a formal marriage. Under this arrangement, Lwin would go live for a year in his wife's home.

Lwin's visits to his fiancée's home became more frequent. On Sundays he would go to town with her family. So the days went by, far from any alien contamination, far from the pompous world of the Ladinos, as the people of Jolomk'u remained isolated behind the mountain walls, growing, multiplying and dying in silence, forgotten.

It was necessary to make public the relationship between the two families by means of the gift of firewood and by a small party organized by Lwin's parents, which should be held in the bride's house a month after the agreement.

Early one morning twenty mules with their polished harnesses and straps headed up the mountain, bathed in sunshine. The men were carrying axes, which had just been sharpened, all ready to bite some ancient tree for the ceremonial wood.

In the village the women scurried to and fro, making the necessary preparations.

Mekel and his son had gone on ahead. In the thick forest they found themselves at the foot of a giant oak, that extended its branches like an old man's arms over the underbrush. The old tree was full of moss, which hung like congealed dew on the branches. Its body was encrusted with a plethora of parasitic plants, flaming *pata de gallo* flowers, orchids opening up their immaculate petals among the branches, ferns that hung down like the tail of a quetzal bird. Little birds of all colors and sizes lived in its branches.

At this hour there was a fiesta of birds, that joined their songs to the peasants' supplications in order to establish direct communication with the Great Spirit there among God's mountains. The candles were burning, lifting the prayers along with the smoke from the incense.

The first woodcutters began to arrive mounted on mules. Their sandals were in the air and there were coils of rope on the harnesses. The animals sprinkled the grass with their breath, bathed in sweat from struggling up the steep slopes.

Lwin blew a horn to tell the men where to go. It should be good firewood. The family's prestige partly depended on it. That tree was just what they needed. They surrounded the tree, which spread out its roots like the veins on a hand grasping the earth. They issued instructions.

Four men simultaneously brandished their axes in the air, which came down to sink their sharp teeth into the great tree. Only a few yellow leaves fell. The arms of the tree drove flocks of birds up into the blue sky, which flew off singing a song of farewell. The sweat of the vigorous youths saturated the coarse shirts under their *capixayes*.

"Four more now," ordered the one directing the work. The others stepped back, wiping off the sweat with their forearms and the nicks on their axes.

So they worked, four at a time, among laughter and jokes, quickly becoming bathed in sweat. The last blows of the axe began to make the tree shake. The last birds evacuated their territory, fluttering over their chicks in the warm nests still standing among the thick leaves.

"Move the animals away," they heard.

"Throw the ropes to the right. Just leave two at the top."

"Watch out! Get back!"

Soon they heard a crunching sound, then a shower of noises like big drops falling on a roof, that grew louder until it exploded under the weight of a hundred tons of years as it fell to earth. Down came a stream of bird's eggs among the *pata de gallo* flowers, lizards and little pigeons with beaks open to receive death, without ever having lived.

For a moment Lwin felt as if he were witnessing a village collapsing under the onslaught of a massacre, flinging hundreds of little Maya into orphanhood: no one's enemy, mute witnesses to the facts, whose only offense is to have been born poor. Like mother birds fluttering around, looking among the debris, their rights had been snatched away from them in the name of a democracy not their own, built according to the wishes of the few. The echo went from tree to tree, from ravine to ravine, frightening the animals of the forest, which fled from the noise pursuing them like Maya fleeing the noise of arms, victims of the ideology of others.

Once the tree was on the ground, more than twenty men fell on it. They would make firewood out of that oak tree. It was the best, the most prestigious kind, for those offering it as part of the marriage proposal for a pretty girl.

Later, the stiff-legged mules went down the hill in a single file, with the firewood on their backs, panting and snorting through the windows of their dilated nostrils The road zigzagged on the face of the steep mountain.

Malin's house had been swept since early morning, and both families awaited the arrival of the woodcutters. It was noon.

"Tie up the dogs," said someone, "here come the men down the hill."

A lad dragged the dogs away, two in each hand, which he tied to a peach tree.

Lwin and his father led the procession. They greeted the

people, who were smoking cigarettes in the entry way, then they unloaded the firewood from the animals. They arrived one after another, and Matin Anton's courtyard and his whole house smelled like vintage oak. The firewood was piling up on the black earth.

As soon as the old men had performed the ceremony, the woodcutters tied up their beasts of burden with loose cinches under the avocado, peach and apple trees or on simple stakes buried in the earth.

The tired men sat on the benches, on the piles of firewood or any place in the shade they could find, and attached themselves to their gourds of drink like children to breasts. The sun burned over the landscape.

The women hurried up their cooking by blowing on the fire.

After washing their hands, they all sat down to eat. In front of those woodcutters who had brought their beasts of burden, two bowls of food were placed, one for the master and the other for the animal.

The ceremony of the gift of firewood was to recognize publicly the nuptial agreement between the two young people. In this ceremony, the parents of the bride enumerated the close relatives to be notified.

Lwin made a list of some two hundred families from different villages who needed to be visited and given the announcement, along with a gourd of corn drink and some cash.

In this first ceremony they arranged the final details of the couple's marriage and agreed that the wedding would take place three weeks hence.

Lwin's relatives entered a stage of even more intense preparation: corn for making *chilate*, clothing for the newlyweds and food preparation. Then there was the money that was to accompany the announcement to each guest, the amount depending on the closeness of the relationship.

They had to get the money ready to give to Malin's parents in recognition for the sacrifices and solicitude involved in their daughter's upbringing.

The days preceding the wedding were very busy.

Mekel had to sell the last of his livestock and a piece of land to cover the costs.

When the day came they filled two hundred gourds with *chilate* and the respective coins and breads so that several boys, previously selected, could go to all the distant villages to distribute them. There were ten boys, members of Lwin's family, some of whom would travel for two days.

The ceremony was held at the home of the bride. Guests and relatives came bringing clothing and tools for the groom. Among those who came were people bringing *chilate*, and the village elders, among whom were the scribe, the diviner, grandfathers and grandmothers.

At Malin's house another group of relatives had gathered.

Malin wore the new outfit her father had bought her. Lwin was dressed up in blue pants, a *capixay* with bright threads, a white hat and crude leather sandals. He brought a set of new clothing for Malin. The women brought three large baskets on their heads containing clothing for the couple.

A loud firecracker went off, just like the day Lwin was born.

"Sit down for a while," invited Matin Anton. "Thank God we woke up without headaches."

"Dear friends," interrupted Mekel, "before beginning our talk together, I want to show you the presents these young people are bringing and at the same time ask permission for them to go to the villages they have been assigned to visit," he said.

"Thank you for your attention," answered Malin's grandfather. "They can go, but first they have to eat a tortilla in the kitchen. The road is long and the sun is hot."

The elders began the ceremony.

The young couple stood next to one another.

In the center of the house, surrounding a table, in front of the wooden crosses, a long dialogue was begun, alternating among the elders. With heads bowed, the couple listened to advice and guidance concerning how to live well according to the norms transmitted orally from generation to generation.

The father of the groom, standing before the most respected elders present, began:

"Friends, to all of you who have come, we give thanks for your presence. Our family has come to bring you a small gift, not as payment for the great sacrifice and diligence that you have shown in the upbringing of your daughter, but only as a humble recognition of the sacrifices which you have had to make."

As he was saying this, Mekel untied a silk handkerchief in which he had a stack of rolled-up bills. He put them on the table in front of all the guests. He licked his fingers and began to count to twenty: the twenty sacred days, that gave strength and virtue to Malin, who was now to have her own mate.

Then, before the community, the women handed over clothing for the bride, kitchen utensils, work tools and personal items.

"Thank you, friends, thank you," replied the bride's father clasping his hands. "From now on, your son is our son. We are happy because our families have united to help the new couple live in the way of work, service and love."

"Ladies and gentlemen," said another important elder, "from this moment on, all of you are responsible for the successes and the failures of this new family. Therefor, you should take care to guide them in family life, so that they will be an example for their descendants, respecting and honoring our race."

"As a token of the acceptance of this great responsibility, from now on you will be considered as relatives."

Everyone shook hands and greeted one another

respectfully, then each elder put his hands on the head of the couple to give them his blessing.

Dinner was served with *kuxa*.

The marimba wafted its notes to the tears of the grandfathers and grandmothers embracing as family members.

Lwin's mother cried as she embraced Malin's mother. She was about to let her son go for a year to another house.

"Don't worry, *comadre*," said Malin's mother. "We'll take good care of him here just as you do at home. He won't lack for corn gruel, clothing or tortillas."

From that day on, Lwin lived in his wife's house.

When the year was over, he returned to his parent's house, along with his wife carrying a child on her back. It was little Lotaxh, wrapped in a checkered cloth with a red cap to avoid the evil eye.

Lwin came back into the bosom of his family for the next stage of his life.

The storm clouds that the old diviner had seen coming up over the horizon soon invaded the sky of Jolomk'u and the whole region. The sky was black, loaded with terror and chills that penetrated everywhere.

The first symptoms of that strange evil showed up at the doors of the most destitute and helpless. Panic stricken, the villagers looked for a place to hide.

Those who had until then savored a bit of brown sugar on Sunday, coffee, salt, and from time to time, a piece of mutton with heaps of tortillas, no longer could do so. The poor became poorer and poorer and the rich became richer.

The farmers were drowning in an sea of desperation. The reduced number of employers and firms that monopolized production kept raising the prices of the most basic items, to way beyond the reach of the Maya.

Corruption at all levels was eating away at the very heart of the country's economy, to the point that reserves reached zero. Politicians and the government were creating conditions that would lead to civil conflict.

The tentacles of other political systems took advantage of the situation to come and shake the sleeping consciousness of the Maya, offering them redemption. Moved by desperation, many took up arms, for in their view it was better for them to die fighting against an unjust and oppressive regime than for them and their children to be vanquished by hunger.

There was no one to impose order in the nation. Each plunderer zealously carried off riches toward his own lair, emptying the national treasury in the process.

The powerful manipulated the laws at will. There were no laws to regulate their conduct or that of their hangers-on. Repression against the populace was more severe every day, to the point that intelligence agents swarmed everywhere. Anyone who tried to protest or demand that their rights be respected was immediately silenced. Intellectuals began a mass exodus. Those that did not manage to escape were buried in clandestine cemeteries or subjected to torture.

It was a nation of the deaf, mute and blind, a mindless flock. That was the only way to stay alive.

The media were conscious of the long daily lists of the dead, up to a point, but those who died in Jolomk'u or in even more remote places were swallowed up in silence.

Every day the Maya took their dead to the cemeteries. With no shroud, no wake, no comment, they buried them in open pits.

Their work was insufficient to feed their children, because of the time spent "voluntarily" patrolling the roads day and night. If they went to the fincas, they had to pay for a replacement in the patrol. The population was constantly harassed by the two warring bands. The Maya not only paid a very high price of many dead, but had no clear understanding of the reasons for the war. They only knew misery, pain, and hunger. They fought not for their own ideas, but for the ideas of others.

Entire villages were massacred by armed men that arrived with savage fury.

Years later, when the war was at its cruelest; when chains of disfigured corpses appeared on the roads; when armed men came down daily from the mountains to take villagers; when no fiestas or meetings of any kind were held; when people went to bed before dark, shutting their doors with double bars, with dogs tied in the entry ways, an officer brought Mekel a notice from the army. The notice carried the saddest possible message for the parents, piercing their hearts like a sword. It said that their son Nikol "had fallen fulfilling his duty in defense of the Fatherland."

They shed tears until their eyes withered from so much crying.

While people were busy picking up their dead, government officials devoted themselves to storing the nation's wealth in more secure places for themselves.

"Why so much pain, dear God?" sobbed Lotaxh.

"Why this conflict between brothers of the same people? What sense does it make to kill one another, impelled by Ladino ideas toying with our lives? We're mere instruments of other men's desire for power."

Nikol's mortal remains were buried in Jolomk'u. Four silent men carried the coffin, followed by a large entourage, mainly women dressed in white.

"Be patient, *comadre*, we're all going to have to go through this," they told Lotaxh, who was sobbing among the women.

"Impossible," she replied. "It would have been better for me to die, for I'm an old woman. Why did it have to be my son in the flower of youth. Dear God, why have you let this happen?"

The murmur of the crowd mixed with the sad melody of an accordion that went ahead of the casket.

They lowered the box with two ropes down into the open grave. Then all threw handfuls of dirt as their last farewell. That grey afternoon, they all went to drink from the sorrow in Lotaxh's maternal heart, which had become a source of bitterness and pain. She rebelled at leaving her son in the midst of the cold loneliness of the dead. She was stretched out over the grave mound.

"Come home, *comadre*, it's already dark," they said.

From then on, she spent her days sunk in solitude. They would often hear her talking to herself any time and any place. Sometimes she cried in silence.

The political problems had become worse. Organizations, labor unions, and cooperatives were dismembered. Their leaders were assassinated and persecuted. Pastors and church workers were put under surveillance. Anyone with a leadership position in the community was watched by both of the fighting factions.

The country was being abandoned by the community of nations. They were converting it into an island of cannibals and savages, where the law of the jungle ruled.

The idea of death had overpowered the people in the form of a collective psychosis. Entire families, complete communities fell under the bullets.

The people fled, abandoning their houses and meager belongings.

Mayan social structure creaked under the weight of political violence. The scaffolding broke under the very feet of the communities unable to find an escape route.

State institutions had lost all ethical values. Laws seemed to be papers blown about the streets of dirty neighborhoods.

Those villagers who would not go up into the mountains of their own free will were forced to flee with their relatives. The children were dying of cold, hunger and illness in the forests. The families that managed to escape spent days and days walking through the mountains and canyons toward distant places, without identity cards, without roads and without a country. Thousands were left wandering around, trying to find a safe place to live, offering their labor as the only merchandise they had.

The most unfortunate buried themselves and their hopes beyond the limits of where they had planted their roots. The politicians, blind to reality, could find no solution to the problems. "Only through dialogue and cooperation can we resolve our differences" shouted the demagogues gesturing with one hand, while with the other they covered the mouths of the masses. They cooperated only with the powerful.

The labor unions, the students, the bureaucrats and the small groups that still remained tried to speak out. But for the millions of Maya, who made up the majority, there was no one to listen to them, no one to speak to them or speak for them. The categories established in life extended beyond the grave. When some Ladino political leader died, it was headlined in the newspapers and other media of communication. But when peasants died, there was only silence. The conscience and the feelings of society created a hard shell of indifference. It didn't arouse any reaction, it had all become routine.

Lwin's fellow student, the one who had gone to school in the city, was to comment much later that, "The State, the sovereign power, which in other climes represents the interests of the majority, worries only about the minority here. They see us with the eyes of Ladinos, listen to us with the ears of Ladinos and speak to us in the language of Ladinos."

"There's a great chasm between this abstract entity and us. We have to build a bridge, not just of vague, sterile words, but of mutual understanding born of good will and sincerity. They have to stop deceiving the people."

"In concrete terms, what is sovereignty?" asked Lwin.

"I would say that it is the sum of the will of the majority of the country's inhabitants," answered Matin Tikxhun.

"My understanding is that the sum of these wills is personified in the men elected by the people to represent and govern them through a system of just laws, not as they do it here," he concluded.

"Yes, this presupposes that they should be faithful servants of the will of the majority that put them in power, looking out for the common good and not merely serving a minority. This is what we call democracy, although it is really more complex than that."

"A political system like that would be worth fighting for at all costs," replied Lwin.

"Of course, Lwin, but unfortunately, that's only in theory or written in the articles of the Constitution. In practice it's constantly trampled on. It's become the heritage of a few who manipulate the hallowed rights of the people, taking advantage of their ignorance and their limited vision of their own reality. These manipulators do whatever they can to get power, not to serve, but to satisfy their own interests. Here the political parties that ought to be sources of ideology to guide the people to look for their own alternative toward development, have become simply electoral instruments to assume power and enrich a few."

"You know, Matin, it's sad to see that because of the ambition of a few, this country is sinking farther and farther each day. God willing, we'll talk of this another day. See you later; it's been a pleasure talking to you."

Mekel had died a few years before. Lotaxh had grown old in poverty and constant illness. She had been stretched out for months on her wooden pallet, hobbled by leg cramps. The burning of incense had no effect. Nor had the hunting of the deer for curative purposes been successful, nor prayers to God on the hills, under the cliffs or on the banks of rivers. The gods had become deaf, both to the language of the Maya and to the prayers of the Ladinos.

The phenomenon of political violence had shattered the economy of the Maya. They were the ones who paid the most for this sad situation. With constant illness, the severity of the war and the bad times for their cornfields, Lwin had to mortgage his last piece of land to get food. The Ladino, who was the only one who had money, would lend him two hundred and fifty quetzales at ten per cent interest per month.

Lwin had to find other places to grow corn, so he could feed his family. To save his father's land from the hands of the loan sharks, Lwin left his village and went for a few months elsewhere where there was land that could be cultivated. He began by felling trees and burning off the underbrush so he could plant corn. They were fertile lands, but in the midst of a virgin forest, far from his village, far from his people

Lwin did not make it home for All Souls' Day that year. Some days before, the women had gone to clear the weeds away and clean up the grave sites at the cemetery.

Grey days went by under a constant drizzle. The squash plants were flowering as the corn brought forth its first fruits. There were furtive bird songs among the bean flowers and the marigolds. The hummingbirds remained suspended in the air with invisible wings sucking the nectar of each flower, as the thin clouds of November crowned the tops of the hills from early in the day.

"What day is today?" asked Lotaxh from her pallet.

"It's the day before All Souls' Day," answered the youngest of her daughters.

"Remember to prepare everything necessary for receiving the spirits of the ancestors," she said haltingly. "They'll come and visit your homes and your children."

"Very well, mother, that's what we'll do."

"Has Lwin returned yet?"

"No. He's coming back in a few weeks. He sent a message that the cornfields gave a good harvest, but that he hasn't found a way to bring the corn because of the bad weather. The roads are full of mud, and the pack animals sink into the swamps. They say a lot of them have died, buried with load and all. It's three days travel and almost no one can get out under those conditions."

"Your poor brother. It would've been better if he hadn't gone."

"Tomorrow prepare the sweat bath with warm water and bunches of flowers for the dead. Make the corn gruel. Cook *ayote* squashes with brown sugar. Put on a pot of chayote and make some tortillas with the new corn, so that the souls won't go away sad. Too bad I'm too old and sick to do it myself."

When the next day dawned, a silent drizzle was falling, soaking the chains of colored paper that adorned the graves. Mekel's two younger sons carried branches of fir and red pine. The shoulder bag was full of marigolds, and other wild flowers. They had gone to buy the candles and the colored paper for decorating the graves. They also brought chayotes, ears of corn, *güicoy* squash, a jug of corn gruel and a bottle of liquor, so that the spirits of the dead could come down and taste the first fruits of their harvest.

The other sister had stayed at home to take care of the sick woman, sweep the house, and prepare the sweat bath as she had been ordered.

The two brothers, a boy of eighteen and his sister, planted candles for each of the family's dead. They set out food beside each grave and sat under the drizzle waiting for the candles to burn.

Later on the sun lit up patches of light on the green village. The clouds, gathering like a flock of birds, flew into the distance.

"Are you the children of my late friend Mekel?" asked a man that had approached them.

"Yes sir, we are," they answered.

"And how is his wife doing?"

"Always sick. She's been in bed for several months."

"Poor thing. Take care of her because she has suffered a lot. Wait for me, I'm going to look for a fiddler to play a piece for my old friend. His soul must be around here somewhere." Having said this, he went looking for the musician.

Soon the man came back with a fiddler and a guitar player.

"Play, boys, here's where my friend is buried. *When the Indian Cries*, please, that was his favorite piece."

The musicians squatted down next to the dancing candle and began to play some notes that always ended in the harsh sounds of sorrow, much like the words of their language. They cried and danced on Mekel's grave, and on Nikol's, which was nearby. Later on, Malin came to burn candles and also to cry, especially over the grave of one of her small children who had died of measles. Then she went to look for the graves of her parents, who had also died.

Boisterous boat-tailed grackles gathered in the cypresses surrounding the cemetery. When the candles were spent, the party said farewell to the dead, then returned home.

Shortly after All Souls' Day, Lotaxh's health worsened. There was no one to take the news to Lwin.

The bad weather continued. That's how things stood when one day a court summons came from the departmental capital addressed to Lwin. It required his prompt appearance in court.

The brother who was still at home went down unknown roads with his bundle on his back, looking for his brother to give him the news. Three days later he found him in the midst of the forest under torrential rains.

"It must be about the loan," said Lwin. A week later they returned covered with mud, emaciated and with empty mules. Two of the mules had become buried in the swamps with all the corn they carried.

"The whole harvest was lost," Lwin told them. "There's no way to get them through the mountains without roads. The animals can't make it."

He had returned defeated once more, with no money, no corn and no animals, desperate in the midst of that swamp that was swallowing up his life.

Two days later he came before the judge.

"Your honor, I've come about the telegram I received."

"Yes, my boy. I called you to tell you that Mr. Marcelo

Castañeda has filed a suit against you. Mr. Castañeda testified before the court that he lent you the sum of one thousand, two hundred and fifty quetzales for three months," said the judge.

"The two of you signed a contract, the terms of which both parties promised to fulfill. And since you have not kept your part of the agreement, the property you offered as collateral has passed into Mr. Castañeda's ownership, plus court costs."

Lwin's face turned pale.

"Your honor," he began, "what you are saying is not so, because neither was it one thousand, two hundred and fifty nor was it three months for repayment. Please let me explain," he said.

"I'm not making this up," said the judge, visibly upset. "I don't live in your town and I don't know what debts you may have incurred. The papers, my boy, that's what counts."

"That's what I want to explain, your honor. I did ask Mr. Castañeda for a loan of two hundred and fifty, at ten per cent monthly interest, to be repaid in six months. It was not at all like you say."

"Secretary!"

"Yes, your honor."

"Bring me the copies of the expropriation papers in favor of Mr. Marcelo Castañeda."

"Yes, sir."

The secretary read the documents. There was Lwin's signature, his identification number and the signature of two more witnesses.

"Do you see, my boy? It's not good to fail the obligations you incur, nor is it good to lie. There is your signature and your particulars. No one is going to make up those things. Furthermore, here are the witnesses, who I suppose are honorable people, which is why you chose them. And if that isn't enough, here are the photocopies of your titles. What I advise you to do is to go and talk with attorney Rodríguez on Amargura Street on the road to the cemetery. Ask for him, everyone knows him and take this little paper so that you can sign the quitclaim deed for Mr. Castañeda. That's to save you another trip later on. The lawyer is a good man, and with this note you won't have any difficulty having your signature accepted."

"Look, judge," said Lwin indignantly. "This is nothing more than another crooked deal among you Ladinos, that are sucking the lifeblood of my people. People like you are the ones who are really responsible for the country going over the brink, because you are creating exactly the right conditions for people to nurture feelings of vengeance. I'm beginning to believe it's better for each man to take justice into his own hands than to wait for help from people like you who are supposed to impart justice. If this can happen with people entrusted with great responsibility, what can you expect of the rest? Now, where do you think I should go to appeal, to another judge? That's all right, do whatever you want, I'm neither the first nor the only Maya despoiled of his goods. The only thing left for me to do is to challenge you before the Divine Judge, who doesn't allow himself to be bribed or to collaborate in the type of injustice that you inflict daily."

"What you're saying is an attack on the sovereignty of the State."

"And what you're doing is genocide against the people that make the State possible."

"Enough! Get out of here," ordered the judge.

"Why don't you remove from your hardened conscience the voice that still reminds you of your misdeeds? Why don't you push to one side the parade of withered faces that causes you nightmares in the night, the faces of little children that die of hunger and cold on account of you?"

"Guards!"

"Yes, sir."

"Take this man away and jail him for three days without food."

"I can go hungry for three or more days, but you, every time you lift food to your mouth, your inner voice which, if you can still hear it, will tell you that you have taken it away from other defenseless people."

These last words he uttered in the large courtyard, at the back of which was the jail.

When he returned to Jolomk'u after three days of not eating, he embraced his bedridden mother and his family that wept next to him. He had seen the naked face of ignominy. He had touched the most profound depths of pain a human being can suffer.

He spent various days absorbed in thought. He worked, he walked, he slept, and he was fed like someone not there. He spoke very little and spent much time alone.

One morning he left the house unexpectedly without his machete and without telling anyone where he was going. He wandered about, with no destination. The hours went by and Lwin did not come back.

He had climbed to the top of that mountain where he had gone with his grandfather when he was a child. There he sat and analyzed the options he could choose for the remainder of his life. Lwin was not a man who had been born to lose. He would move ahead despite these problems. He wanted to fight on for his family and his community and was looking for the most appropriate way.

Various possibilities rose to consciousness, and he analyzed them one by one. Thus passed hours in meditation. As evening fell he came down from the mountain, finding comfort in the warmth of his own people.

Lwin had finally discovered something very important. Many years' experience had shown him that the people of Jolomk'u had many problems, and that if each one tried to solve them on his own, they would never succeed.

He well knew that the consequences of each attempt were more disappointment, until people gave up trying to resolve their problems. In view of this reality he began the most difficult task of his life. That's when his hair began to turn to grey.

He sought out people, spoke with them, went from house to house, insisted, begged, reproached and even implored people to listen to him.

"You're dreaming, Lwin," they replied. "Our fathers have lived for hundreds of years in this place and for all generations life for us has always been the same: suffering." They shook their heads and turned back to their dull life in the shadows.

Years of fight and persuasion went by. But Lwin persisted with his plan, convinced that some day people would change.

"We're like scattered bees each trying to construct its own beehive," he said to them. "Look at the tiny ants doing great things. Why not unite our minds and our strength to save ourselves? One by one, we'll never get very far."

Little by little the doubters approached to listen to what Lwin had to say. They came very hesitantly.

When there was a large enough group, Lwin began the first stage of his grand plan. They would meet in different homes in the evenings after work, on weekends or on holidays.

"What's happening to the people of Jolomk'u?" he asked them. "Speak up, speak of your own failures, your pain and your suffering. The act of sharing with others can be a relief in itself," he said.

They began to tell of the death of children, the sickness of loved ones, of animals, of the loss of harvests, of lands. Each and every thing from the past and the present were falling into a gunny sack of common memories.

Lwin presented his own life experiences. The experiences of each family and each person were taken into account in their list of experiences.

Little by little, more and more people came together, at first to listen and then to participate. Besides the respect that existed in the community, a real friendship arose among neighbors. From the state of complaints and sorrow in which most were submerged, they rose into an atmosphere of smiles and happiness, product of the strength they received in their semiweekly meetings.

Later there were requests for more meetings in people's homes. Generally, they ended very late, but the men and women attended with interest and enthusiasm.

When Lwin thought the time was right, he made a summary of all of the problems that had been described by the villagers. It was an endless list of real events that had been presented by the people themselves: from the collective problems that affected everyone to particular problems of each family and each person.

"This is the inventory of what we have in our treasury," he said when he presented a list. "We're extremely poor, ignorant, our children die, they take away our lands. We don't have good crops, we don't have adequate education, our animals die, we come down with a lot of illnesses. Religious and political systems, and still other systems confuse us. They make us ashamed of ourselves, our roads are bad, our water is too far away, we are in darkness, we don't have means of communication and transportation, we use leather carrying straps to carry our things. We don't have a way of protecting ourselves from the cold or the heat and from bad weather. They deceive us, steal from us, discriminate against us, and exploit us. Our crafts and our work are difficult and take a long time to finish. We don't have the technology needed to speed up our production. Our forests are disappearing more and more. Our lands are losing their fertility. Our cultural values, languages and our clothing are dying out more each day. Our work is not well paid. We relieve our sorrows by alcoholism." So he continued enumerating each and every one of those experiences.

"If we look beyond Jolomk'u," he continued, "we must admit in sadness that our country is one of the most backward in the world. Many people like us are isolated in these mountains where basic services don't exist. We Maya make up more than sixty per cent of the total population, but we occupy only a small percentage of the total area of the country. Our lands are also the least productive and the poorest in the country. Families subsist mainly on corn. Our small parcels have been split up as the population grows at a high rate, one of the highest in the world. We're facing the highest population growth and the lowest low per capita income."

"Our economy is based on agriculture and some crafts with few resources, not really enough to feed, clothe, educate and provide medical attention for our large families."

"We Maya make up twenty-one different linguistic communities, each with its own dress and life style, living in the same territory with uniform laws and norms. We can't communicate with one another, we can't agree, since we're not integrated."

"A large percentage of the population is illiterate, made

up mainly of us Maya. Very few of our children attend elementary school, for they lack a preparatory stage which would allow for a transition period between the home and the school. Four-fifths of our young people have no access to intermediate education. Higher education is just a dream for us."

"The content of the curriculum, the educational methods, the procedures and the evaluation systems aren't adapted to our needs nor are our expectations appropriate for our heterogeneous society with its different realities.

"Eighty-five per cent of those that manage to enter elementary school drop out during the first few years. Fifty per cent repeat grades."

"What are the real reasons for these failures?

"We don't really know."

"What we can be sure of is that we receive an urban education, although we live in a culturally-different rural area.

"Because of the accelerated population growth, the average life expectancy among us is less than sixty years."

"Death and illness rates among our children are high, because of the scourge of measles, whooping cough, parasites, respiratory illnesses and malnutrition."

"We are counted among the major consumers of alcohol, a means of escape from so many problems, but we put ourselves in an even more poverty-stricken state, in which it becomes harder and harder to survive."

After enumerating these problems and experiences, there was a long silence, and many wept, commiserating with each other.

"Well," said Lwin. "I got you together just to present this information. Now you can all go home, I won't bother you any more," he said. Silence reigned once more.

After a long while:

"No!" said a woman. "No!" said others with emotion tying up their throats and tears silently falling.

"What do you want?" he asked.

"Don't leave us, Lwin," they begged. "There has to be something more, we can find it among ourselves, this is just the beginning."

"Do you want to go on?" he asked again.

"Yes!" they all answered.

"But what comes next is something for brave men and women, for fighters that won't give up in the face of defeat, no matter how painful."

After a brief silence and looking severely at all the other peasants there, Lwin went on: "The time is past for crying, feeling sorry for ourselves, and walking with bowed head and our arms forming a cross. People of Jolomk'u, let's go bury these things and wake up, for the greatest task we have to face is yet before us. The cry-babies, those too weak to fight, those who are content with their lot in life, the bored and the lazy, we don't need you. Keep your boredom and conformity. There won't be any leaders among us, no one higher than another; just the strength of our collective wills can make success possible."

"Let's go, Lwin! Guide us in this struggle," shouted every one.

During the next few months they made an intense analysis of each one of the problems that had been presented.

"What do you think about our problems?" Lwin asked each one, from the youngest to the oldest. "What is the point of view of each one of you and how do you feel in the depths of your hearts and your soul? Declare all your feelings and your most intimate thoughts about our common life."

Some expressed the feeling that those problems had them sunken in backwardness, made life harsh and difficult for them, forgotten in the midst of their sufferings without the respite enjoyed by most people. "It's hard living like this," they said.

"What do you feel about what's really happening to us?"

Lwin asked them.

Some answered: "We feel pain, we are sad to see our little ones malnourished and our sick children die, without being able to do anything to prevent their death. We feel insignificant in our ignorance, not knowing a lot of things that there are to know, and with us separated from them. Our hands and minds are empty of knowledge. We're defeated. We're desperate. Disabled like orphans without protection. In our lives there is silence, emptiness, pain and need."

"What do you feel seeing others suffer?"

"We feel compassion, pity, sadness, pain, anguish at our inability to help them, sometimes hatred and bitterness against those who foster these things with their indifference and complicity."

Everyone spoke, men and women, all expressing what they felt.

"Brothers and sisters, now that you have spoken, I wish to speak," Lwin said. "All of the problems that you have mentioned and that are listed on this sheet, as well as others that we haven't mentioned, are the result of something. All have an origin and a reason; they are not the products of chance or luck."

"All of us together have to look for the causes in the next stage of our work. When we are working in the fields and we get a thorn in our foot, this causes us a lot of pain. Many times it produces an infection if we don't take the thorn out. The same thing happens with problems. They have a origin and a cause that comes either from ourselves or from forces outside of ourselves."

"Why do you think that our children die?"

"Because it's God's will," some answered. "Because that is our fate," said others.

"Good, later on we'll see if that's true."

"Why do you think we are poor?" he asked.

"Because we're dumb," said some.

Thus he continued to ask about each of the problems presented during the evening meetings the community held over several weeks. The causes of illness, the poor yield of the land, the scarcity of water, the death of animals, the poor roads, the uncomfortable houses, poverty, deception by politicians, lawyers, economists, cultural leaders. Everyone participated, each one presented his own point of view.

"You have given a lot of reasons," he continued. "Some of these reasons are valid and others are not. Of two things I'm sure. Our problems are not due to our being stupid, nor is it God's will that we lead this kind of life. What is happening, my friends, is that we haven't had the opportunity to develop our abilities and our potential. That's why we're ignorant of a lot of things and this ignorance keeps us in these conditions. But we can overcome it and that is the direction our efforts should take. Because the development of peoples is not achieved by passing out weapons to the citizens so that they can exterminate one another, but rather allowing them access to a liberating education that isn't exclusively for the elites."

"Two more questions," said Lwin. "First, what have we done until now?"

"Cry, get drunk, give up hope, accept our fate, sit down to wait for death, stretch out our hands to passersby to ask them for leftovers, grovel in front of those who have something, beg, follow false leaders who take us over the precipice and to death."

"And what do we do now?" pondered Lwin.

The crowd did not know what to answer. They stayed silent, looking at each other. They weren't used to this kind of reflection. They had never had answers to their problems; never had they found the way out of the labyrinth of the lives they led, sunken in the darkness of ignorance.

"What shall we do, Lwin?" they asked.

"What we should do, friends, is start right here and now. We can't wait for people to come from the outside to bring us a shirt that doesn't fit. Let's weave our own shirts with our own threads, our own strength and our own designs, our own colors, to our own tastes. Shirts made to order for other people will never fit us."

"Yes," everyone said. "Let's work, but how?"

"Let's go back." said Lwin. "Let's start with the very first problem, and go over the long list hanging on the wall in this room. Let's see which is first and which follows. What are the problems that affect us the most and how do they affect us? From the child to the senior, we all have a role to play here," he told them.

They began to prioritize the problems in the order of the real interests of the community. For each one they looked for concrete solutions. They set goals, they laid out objectives, they estimated the resources available to carry them out and set a time limit for each action.

Priority was given to the physical and biological care of children, within their means. They oriented them in their intellectual, psychological and social development so that a new generation could grow with the values and aspirations of the group. They wanted to lay the foundations of self-development, planting a seed in each person. The most relevant group was obviously that of the children taking their first steps in that new world.

"Let's cultivate our children as carefully as we cultivate our cornfields," said Lwin. "so they will be successful intellectually and socially."

"Let's work our lands, using what we need, looking for the necessary ingredients for adequate growth. We'll all work together to mold the behavior and values of our children. We have to cultivate vegetables and fruit and raise animals. We don't know how to do it, but we should look for someone to guide us in improving these activities," they decided.

They formed committees, organized the community, assigned responsibility and tasks. Then trainers in different fields began to arrive in Jolomk'u for various lengths of time to develop the knowledge and skills of the villagers.

"We should know and transform our environment and our world," they said.

Many of the literate village youth were sent to receive training and then came back to the community.

A group of people knowledgeable in different areas was formed: health, agriculture, community organization, manufactures and technology adapted to the needs, characteristics and aspirations of the local population.

Lwin made frequent trips to visit offices, ministries, embassies, and different specialists to bring to his people what was beneficial to them. They were thirsty for knowledge more than for money. They tried to avoid any material gifts. They wanted to learn to make things rather than receive them ready made. The women received training in child care, hygiene, food preparation, the care of their homes.

They managed to build a school in the community. It was built by everyone and came to be a development center for the people. Meetings were held in the large school hall, where they also set up workshops and laboratories, where people put into practice the knowledge they had acquired. They looked for scientific explanations for natural phenomena, and starting from their own experience they generated projects and concrete action.

They worked night and day.

They welcomed experts from different fields, allowing them to be there only as long as necessary to transmit their experience and knowledge. They didn't want to become dependent on them.

Later they set up a town library, where people could go to read in their free time and entertain themselves with organized recreation, using the games and amusements of their own culture.

The older ones entertained the children, telling them about

the lives they had led, thus strengthening the foundation of a collective feeling of unity and social cohesion.

Sports became popular, formerly regarded as a waste of time.

As the years went by, the darkness of the village was dispelled by an electrification project. The pitch pine torches were put away, the candles taken down from the walls. Water was brought in from a distance to clean the dirty facades of the houses and alleviate the thirst of the land, in order to germinate various seeds, filling the face of the earth with greenery. Literacy passed from being a means of alienation and instrument of exploitation to an instrument of progress for the peasants, who walked the path of letters toward self-understanding. Opportunists wasted no time seeking out Lwin to offer him the job of mayor, knowing that the people trusted him.

"Thank you very much," he said, "but I still have a lot of work to do here in Jolomk'u." Later on he would note, "No one gives something for nothing. They won't share their monopoly of power if they don't get a hundred-to-one return. The political hacks just try to satisfy their own ambitions and aren't interested in the progress of our villages. They have been blinded by self-interest for so long, that they are unable to suggest an ideological and philosophical basis of life that is adequate for us. Nor are they interested in doing so."

They kept on working.

"We don't believe in abstract religions that forget man," they answered the shouting soapbox speakers. "If man is in the image of this God you are preaching about, first let's improve the image of man, so he can clearly recognize God in his own mentality and spirituality."

As their eyes began to open, as their consciousness began to clear, they were finding their way to God, from whom they had become estranged. They nailed images of dark-skinned Christs with Mayan features on their grandparents' crosses.

They loudly proclaimed credos about man and his humanization. They sang canticles and hymns of praise in an eloquent Mayan tongue. They celebrated ceremonies, rites, masses at the dusted-off altars. They pulled out the weeds that grew on the rock altars and stretched out linen cloths along with the straw mats to offer the products of their labor amid the smoking dregs of a sad past.

They understood that systems are created to serve people, not people to serve systems. They were not satisfied with 'micro' enterprises, 'mini' irrigation, informal education, small landholdings, small industries, microplanning, or a third rate society. Instead, they demanded and were conscious of being capable of managing macro enterprises, macro industries. They were participants in the macro economy, having the right to learn and adapt all kinds of technology to their needs and interests because they knew they were the majority, they were a people.

Lwin was so absorbed in the world of his projects that he was unaware that he had passed over the threshold of old age. One morning, when he was sunning his cramps in his flower-filled courtyard, he heard Mayan music as he fixed his gaze on the infinite. A group of grandchildren played with a puzzle depicting Itzamna and grandmother Ixchel in the underworld of Xib'alb'a. Another group of boys played at deciphering the secrets of the stelae by means of some formulas they had discovered. It was a dream.

Then came the white-haired elders and carried Lwin's spirit to the starry heavens to contemplate from the dwelling of God and the sacred days the future of his people.

He saw his people busying themselves with art, science and different technologies. The huts with mud walls had become houses with bright colors. Green fields covered formerly arid lands. The carrying straps fell from the heads of the men to be changed into motorized transport vehicles. It was no longer necessary to hunt down men for the army.

The army came to them to train their bodies and minds. There was no storm or earthquake to move the foundations of the Fatherland, for each brick, each stone had been laid by the citizens, Maya and Ladino alike.

Thousands of men and women of all colors harmoniously joined forces to construct a great monument, a great pyramid built to the heights of other nations.

Lwin returned from the world of the spirit as the sunset of his life approached. A short while later, when Lwin was bringing in the last of his sheaves to the granaries of the gods, when patches of red came down through the skylight of the heavens at sunset, he set out on the last lap of his journey, after having paved the way ahead for his people.

The old man had been in bed for three days. Fever had left him flat on his back, his breathing was labored and irregular. Neighbors and relatives arrived with their little pots of food: chicken soup and children's sized tortillas, made especially for the sick.

"Come on in, sit down," said the women to the people arriving. "The doctors can't explain his resistance, they say he's made of oak."

Several days before people walking the trails had begun to see an old wolf roaming around nearby. They saw him just off the trails, they saw him on the rocks, they saw him by day and heard him at night. His howls were mournful, like those of someone leaving home. No one harmed him, knowing that old Lwin was sick and it could be his *nawal*.

Injections and medicine could not lower the fever. They put cloths wet with lime water on his forehead, but they quickly dried. They washed his feet in water in which the corn dough had been cooked, but the water turned lukewarm. He no longer ate anything. He thirsted only for the water from cooked chayote and corn gruel.

"*Compadre*, what's happening to you?"

"Drink something, even if it's just this bit of soup, don't

leave us."

"There are a lot of events planned, and we're expecting you."

"Mmmm," and he opened his eyes with which he could see a distant world. His mouth was dry and his pulse agitated.

Faces were grave, people looked worried and were tongue-tied with emotion. On a stove where once stood the hearth where old Lwin's umbilical cord was buried, there were now pewter and china dishes, and porcelain pots with food that the people had brought. They had not been touched.

A howl was heard far from the house. Their hair stood on end. The children buried their faces in their parents' arms. The big clock in the room struck eleven.

"Light another candle, one of the big ones. Grandmother is going to pray to the souls," they said.

All of the lights of the house were on, as women and men spoke in low voices throughout the house. They heard the howl again, this time nearer.

"Did you hear that?"

"Yes, it's been around here for three days."

Some women cried silently at the sick man's bed.

"His fever has gone up, bring the thermometer," said the nurse, Lwin's granddaughter.

"Call the doctors," another person advised.

"No! No!" the sick man began to say in his delirium. "No, teacher, don't hit me, it's not my fault," he said. "Don't be so mean. Let me eat my tortillas. Don't take them away from me."

"Let him eat," someone pleaded.

"No. It's been three days since he's had food," they answered.

By dawn he was in deep slumber. The others also managed to sleep a bit. The entire community was gathered in the large house, as though it were their own house. The men took turns hugging the sick man, holding him for a moment as though they wanted to hold back his life for a little longer.

When day broke no one wanted to go home. Everyone was concerned for the health of the man who had shown them the way to success, and had changed their destiny.

At mid-morning his mind was clear for a moment.

"Where's Lukaxh?" he asked.

"Here I am, father."

"Don't cry." And he put his hand on his head. "And your brothers and sisters?

"Here they are, we're all here."

"Don't cry!" he said, and then once again was overcome by drowsiness.

No one spoke.

As the rays of sunlight came in obliquely through the door of the house, they could see the old wolf walking toward the west, silhouetted against a horizon covered by red clouds. His shadow was agitated by the light of the setting sun, and they heard him howl again.

"There they come, it's them. Hide the girls!" he said in his delirium.

"Let ... there ... not ... be ... any ... group ... that ... gets ... left ... behind."

After a long while, he died.

The day was Thirteen Ajaw.

Glossary of Q'anjob'al and Spanish Terms

A Note on Mayan Numerals and the Mayan Calendar

GLOSSARY OF
Q'ANJOB'AL AND SPANISH TERMS

Ajaw	day of the Mayan calendar.
ajtz'ib'	scribe or secretary.
alucema	a medicinal herb.
amargura	bitterness.
Anton	Antonio.
Atanasio Tzul	K'iche' leader who rebelled against the Spanish. He was crowned King of Totonicapán, but his reign lasted only three days.
ayote	a type of squash, with medicinal qualities, *Cucurbita pepo*.
B'en	day of the Mayan calendar.
cacaxte	type of box formed by a framework of sticks, used for carrying burdens.
caldera	cauldron.
ceiba	kapok tree, *Ceiba pentandra*, the national tree of Guatemala, and sacred to the Maya.
capixay	thick jacket woven of black wool, with unused broad sleeves (the arms stick out through slits in the sides). Used in the cold highlands of northwestern Guatemala.
centavo	a hundredth of a quetzal.
chicha	drink made from fermented grain; distilled to make brandy.
chilacayote	a type of squash, *Cucurbita ficifolia*.
chilate	drink made from toasted corn, chile and cacao.
chilca	bush with leaves of medicinal value, *Thevetia nereifolia*.
chocoyo	type of parrot, *Coronus holochlorus*.
colinabo	edible wild vegetable, eaten cooked, *Brassica oleracea napobrassica*.

comadre	mother of one's godchild or godmother of one's child; in extended meaning, 'friend.'
compadre	father of one's godchild or godfather of one's child; in exended meaning, 'friend.'
copal	often referred to by its Mayan name, *pom*, it is an incense made from the gum of the copal tree (*Copal cuauhitl*, *Rhus copallidium*, or *Stemmadenia nobilis* Benth.
costumbre	the syncretistic religion derived from a blend of the ancient Maya religion and sixteenth century Spanish Catholicism, and still practiced by many traditional Maya.
curandero	native healer, who cures with herbs, massage, etc.
don	title of respect for man, normally used with first name
doña	title of respect for woman, normally used with first name.
Elab'	day of the Mayan calendar.
Elnan	Hernández, Fernando.
finca	plantation.
güicoy	a type of squash, *Cucurbita aurantia*.
güipil	long pullover blouse, with wide neckline and short sleeves, worn by Mayan women.
Imox	day of the Mayan calendar.
Iq'	day of the Mayan calendar
Itzamna	creator deity, lord of day and night, inventor of writing and books.
Ixchel	godess of healing, childbirth and divination
Jolomk'u	lit., head of the sun.
Kab' Tz'in	two famous rocks where a pair of lovers, *Kab'* and *Tz'in*, plunged to their death and turned to stone.
kanac	tree, leaves of which are used to wrap up tamales, *Gilibertia arborea*.

Katal	Catarina, Catalina.
kumare	Mayan for *comadre*, q. v.
kuxa	illegal liquor.
Lamon	Ramón.
Ladino	Spanish-speaking dominant group in Guatemala, mainly of mixed Spanish-Indian. ancestry
Lapin	ancient Q'anjob'al surname.
Lolen	Lorenza.
Lotaxh	Rosa.
Lwin	Pedro.
Maltin	Martín.
Matalb'atz	Q'eqchi' leader taken before King Ferdinand of Spain, and given two bells to assist in the evangelization of his people. He broke one, and refused to carry out his assignment, preferring to become a hermit.
Matin	Mateo.
mandamiento	forced labor decreed by the government, for the Maya only.
Mekel	Miguel.
milpa	cornfield.
mimana'	big river.
Mulu'	day of the Mayan calendar.
municipio	the unit of local government, consisting of the central village and the surrounding countryside. The primary focus of local identity for the Maya.
nawal	a person's alter ego; a person who turns into an animal or a thing; a person's spirit or soul; phantoms or evil spirits that roam in the mist.
Nikol	Nicolás.
Nolaxh	Nolasco.
ox q'in	fiesta to honor a baby the third day after birth (lit. fiesta of the third day).

pacaya	palm tree with edible fruit; the leaves are used in fiesta decorations, *Chamaedorea tepejolote*.
Paltol	Bartolo.
patas de gallo	flowering parasitic plant growing on trees.
pepián	a sauce made from tomato, chile, onion, garlic, sesame seed, squash seed, and tomatillo.
pericón	an aromatic, medicinal herb, type of wild marigold, *Tajetes lucida*.
Petlon	Petrona.
pinol	corn drink cooked without sugar.
quetzal	the unit of currency in Guatemala, until the 1970's equal to one U. S. dollar. In late 1994 it was equal to about $0.17. Named after the national bird.
ranchera	Mexican country-style music, very popular in Guatemala.
señorita	young lady, miss.
son	slow, rhythmic, traditional Mayan dance; also means 'music' and 'marimba' in Q'anjob'al.
Sti'ch'en	lit., at the mouth of the cave.
súchil	frangipani.
susto	technically known as 'magical fright,' it refers to an illness caused by a sudden frightening experience.
Tekum Umam	leader of the K'iche' forces against Pedro de Alvarado, conqueror of Guatemala; killed in battle 1524; symbol of Mayan resistance.
Tikxhun	Diego-Juan.
Torol	Dolores.
Tox	day of the Mayan calendar.
Tumaxh	Tomás.
tz'ite	seeds of the *pito* tree, *Erythrina corallodendron*, that look like red beans; used for divining.
tzolkin	ceremonial year with each of the 20 day names

	occurring 13 times (= 260 days).
vos	second-person pronoun, used only with intimates or social inferiors.
Wachwena'	a hill from which the village of Soloma can be seen.
Winaq	man, twenty. 13 Winaq represents 13 x 20, the completion of the 260 days of the tzolkin.
Xhapin	Sebastián, Sebastiana.
Xheka	unleavened wheat roll flavored with anise.
Xhulin	Salvador.
Xhunik	Juan.
Xhuxhep	José.
Xib'alb'a	the Mayan underworld.
Yaxantaq	Green Forest.
Yulch'en	a cave (lit. 'in the rock').

A NOTE ON MAYAN NUMERALS
AND THE MAYAN CALENDAR

As the contemporary Maya rediscover the civilization of their ancestors, they are reviving the use of some of its most notable features, for example, using Mayan numerals with pride to number pages, chapters or section numbers in books, and using date books to keep their appointments in which the days are marked according to the Mayan calendar as well as the Gregorian.

Mayan numerals are based on a vigesimal, rather than a decimal system. (Apparently the ancient Maya decided to use their toes as well as their fingers for counting!) Numeral systems using place to indicate the power of the numbers, and the use of zero, were invented only twice in human history, once by the ancient Hindus and once by the ancient Maya. Thus while the western place system represents 1 - 10 - 100 - 1,000, etc., the Mayan system represents 1 - 20 - 400 - 8,000. Mayan numerals are placed either from bottom to top or from right to left, with a dot representing 1 and a bar representing 5. Thus, for example, 11 is ≐ or ·||. Notice the number on the opposite page: 235 = (11 x 20) + (3 x 5).

The 260-day ceremonial calendar is virtually the only segment of the very complex ancient Mayan calendrical system still in daily use among Maya today. It has been passed on by oral tradition for thousands of years, as well as being inscribed on the great archeological monuments and nowadays on printed calendars and date books. It has great importance in the divination practices of contemporary Mayan priests. This calendar, usually known by its name in Yukatek Mayan, *tzolkin*, consists of a cycle of 20 day names or gods and 13 numbers, such that a given god and a given number will occur only once in 260 days. The order of the day names in Q'anjob'al Maya, the native language of the characters in *A*

Mayan Life, is as follows: Imox, Iq', Watan, K'ana', Ab'ak, Tox, Chej, Lamb'at, Mulu', Elab', B'atz', Eyub', B'en, Ix, Tz'ikin, Kîxkab', Chinax, Kaq, Ajaw. Thus, for example, 3 Imox is followed by 4 Iq', then 5 Watan, etc., much like Tuesday the 5th being followed by Wednesday the 6th, except that there is no beginning day name. In fact the creation of the world (there have been several of them) is dated at 4 Ajaw. Certain days are considered to be lucky, unlucky, or appropriate for certain activities. 13 Ajaw, the most significant day in the life of Lwin, is considered to be the best day of all.